GALAXY GAMES

The Amorphous Assassin

Greg R. Fishbone

Spellbound River

Spellbound River Press

spellboundriver.com

Spellbound River Press
PO Box 1084
Socorro, New Mexico 87801
spellboundriver.com

ISBN: 978-1- 945017-11- 7 (paperback)
ISBN: 978-1- 945017-12- 4 (digital edition)

Library of Congress Control Number: 2016955408

For Dori, Alexi, and Jaida.

Galactic thanks to the Groton Critters
and my friends in the SCBWI.

BY GREG R. FISHBONE

TU BOOKS / LEE & LOW BOOKS:

The Challengers

SPELLBOUND RIVER PRESS:

The Amorphous Assassin

The Mad Messenger (Coming in 2017)

1

BEIJING, CHINA:

A formation of tigersharks burst through the nighttime haze over the Chinese capital. Three streaks of black and orange buzzed past skyscrapers, swept through Tiananmen Square, and rippled the waters of the Zhongnanhai lakes. Before Tyler met M'Frozza, such an event would have whipped up a civilization-shaking, newscaster-screaming, city-burning panic. Now people just watched, pointed, and shared their videos online.

The three tigersharks dove over the rim of an empty Beijing National Stadium, and slid to a stop under the bright lights of the running track. Twin engines spun down on each shark's front spoiler like pairs of hypnotic hammerhead eyes. Pops and hisses sounded like ten thousand soda cans as each shark's door unsealed and dropped open like a set of jaws.

One at a time, thirty-six of Earth's greatest young athletes stepped out—plus one completely ordinary Japanese-American boy from Platte Bluff, Nevada.

Tyler Sato squared his shoulders and raised his chin into the brave front he'd been holding for two-and-a-half years, ever since that crazy week when he'd turned eleven, met an alien squid-girl, and won Earth its first-ever slot in the Galaxy Games Tournament. Billions of fans thought Tyler was the greatest kid athlete in human history, and who was he to tell Earth's entire population that they've got it all wrong?

As Tyler gazed up at the Olympic stadium's steel-banded rim and thought more about what an elite sports hero he wasn't, a teammate accidentally bumped him from behind. As Tyler tumbled to the turf, his brain registered dark skin, frizzy brown hair, and red-rimmed eyes.

It could have only been Weez.

The Brazilian soccer star stooped to help Tyler back to his feet. "Oh, Captain! I'm so sorry. I should watch where I'm going, but I was just thinking about . . . well, you know."

"Your brother?" Tyler asked, as if Weez ever thought about anyone or anything else.

Weez fielded a soccer ball that some practical joker had aimed at his head. The ball dropped from his forehead to his chest, to his knee, to his foot, and stayed there as Weez spun around on his other foot. He fired the ball back the way it had come, all while keeping the same moony-moody expression on his face. "Gustavo would have loved this stadium," he told Tyler. "The Bird's Nest. You know, there was a nest in outside Gustavo's bedroom window. We watched it every day in the spring and summer before—"

Weez tilted his head toward the heavens.

Tyler took off his baseball cap and looked upward with Weez through a respectful moment of silence. "Before your brother was abducted by aliens?"

Weez let out a long breath. "Yeah. And probably for some crazy game show, too."

Tyler shook his head. After M'Frozza and her Mrendarian crew made their official First Contact visit to Earth, another alien race, the Ossmendians, confessed to popping by over the centuries to film a reality show called *Those Wacky Humans*. In classic episodes, ancient peoples had been tricked into building Stonehenge, domesticating cats, or using fossilized dinosaurs as a fuel source, all for the entertainment of an alien audience.

But even Stonifer, the Ossmendians' obnoxious granite slab of a Galaxy Games Captain, had sworn on a stack of bedrock that no humans had ever been stolen away into space. "Have you ever tried to sneak a human into your luggage?" Stonifer had asked. "They wriggle like maniacs, and trust me, you'd never get them past the customs inspectors."

"Stonifer's a jerk, but he's got a strong sense of honor—" Tyler started, but Weez cut him off.

"You and Stonifer have that whole captain-to-captain thing going on, but I don't trust the guy as far as I could throw ten tons of living rock. Which isn't very far, in case you were wondering."

"So you blame the Ossmendians for taking your brother?"

Weez sighed up at the sky. "No. Their ships don't match the one I saw that night. It's got to be the grays." Weez wandered off, still looking up, and bumping into other players along his meandering path. "Sorry. Sorry, dude. Oops. Didn't see you there."

"He's like an apology robot programmed for maximum clumsy," said Tomoko, appearing suddenly at Tyler's side. That had been awkward enough back when they were eleven and she was just a tall Japanese girl with a few masterful judo moves. But since then, Tomoko had sprouted skyward and picked up belts and honors in a half-dozen additional disciplines, while Tyler had very clearly done neither.

Tyler pulled himself onto a low wall at the outside

edge of the track, to create some distance from Tomoko as much as to put them eye to eye. "I feel bad for Weez," he told her. "He lost his brother. Even if aliens didn't take him, that's still got to be tough."

Tomoko rolled her eyes. "Hunter-Elf Zeita lost her brother, too. The dragons got him! The difference is, she didn't get all crazy about it."

"No, the difference is that she's an anime character."

Tomoko glared. "So?"

A cloud of steam poured from Tomoko's ears like she was an angry Mrendarian. It had to be Tyler's imagination, but when he rubbed his eyes, the light gray wisps remained clearly visible beyond her violet-stained pigtails against the empty seats on the other side of the stadium bowl.

Tomoko flicked a finger playfully on his forehead, almost knocking him from his perch. *"Tyler-san no baka!* You don't have to look at me like I'm crazy. Hunter-Elf Zeita is a positive role model whose adventures provide valuable lessons applicable to all aspects of life. It says so on her website."

"She's Tinker Bell with a longbow," Tyler countered.

"Slander!" Tomoko plucked an elf-shaped keychain from her belt loop and covered its tiny pointed ears.

5

"Don't listen to Captain Sato-san. He doesn't know you like I do. He hasn't even finished the third season!"

Tomoko moved away, and Tyler could see that the steam hadn't been coming from her head, but from a tangle of pipes that covered an industrial-ugly pyramid of metal out in the middle of the grass playing field.

Tyler had seen a pyramid like that once on a video screen in Geneva, during a meeting of UNOOSA, the United Nations Office for Outer Space Affairs. The same meeting where Tyler fell asleep during a presentation, and *#NappingTyler* was trending before he'd even woken up. A picture of Tyler's head, face-down on a desk in a puddle of drool, had been the most-Googled image of the year.

For some reason, Tyler had never been invited back to another UNOOSA meeting.

To keep from ruining anyone's surprise, Tyler kept quiet about the pyramid as the other players hung out, goofed off, kicked soccer balls, tossed Frisbees, and did all the other things they always did while waiting for Coach Graham to show up.

On the running track, a pale girl with prominent buck teeth pushed a pair of amber goggles into her blond bangs and struck a pose for a section of imaginary spectators. "All hail Maja Fredriksson, Viking of the Slopes! And the crowd *goes wild!*"

Maja's exclamation in Norwegian echoed back and forth across the empty stadium, and was rendered into overlapping English by the language implant inside Tyler's skull. *"Goes wild! Goes wild! Goes wild!"*

For all her gale-force bluster, Maja was a toothpick-thin wisp who barely filled out a down parka. And yet, she'd assembled a small gang of fellow players who trailed her like a litter of puppies: a Russian swimmer named Valya; a Kuwaiti golf prodigy named Bader; and Indian parkour traceur named Hari; a Greek sprinter named Althea; and an Argentine acrobat who liked to be called "The Amazing Waldo."

On a publicity tour through Scandinavia, the media had dubbed them "Maja's Mob" and the name had stuck, mostly because Maja insisted on using it so often.

The Mob followed Maja toward a knot of players. "Hey, Maja fans! Let's give it up for our good buddy Conor O'Roarke, a master of rugby and Gaelic football—not one, but two completely useless sports!"

Valya and Althea cheered, Hari and Bader high-fived, and the Amazing Waldo hooted like a barn owl.

Conor looked up from his warm-up stretches. "Aye. Too bad you've only got the one useless sport. Plank-standing, is it?"

"Snowboarding," Maja sniffed.

"Give it any fancy name you want. At the end of the day, you're still just standing on a plank."

Maja narrowed her eyes. "At the end of the day, I'd rather be standing on a plank at the center of everyone's attention than being buried under a scrum of sweaty rugby dudes."

Conor clenched his fists and simmered as Maja's Mob danced around him. "Burned!" Hari shouted. "Owned," Bader added. Valya and Althea sang a taunting song while the Amazing Waldo just kept shouting, "Bam!" and throwing out rude hand gestures.

Tyler wanted to step in, but found a firm hand on his shoulder. He looked up at Felix, a boy who was big enough to be a sumo wrestler if he'd been born in Japan. But since he was born in Germany, Felix goal-tended soccer instead. "She's baiting you, Tyler. You know how Maja hates authority figures."

"I'm no authority figure," Tyler scoffed.

"You're our captain. Coach isn't here yet, so you're it. Maja wants to draw you into a fight, but it's not worth it. Conor can take care of himself."

Tyler nodded. Felix made a lot of sense. And sure enough, after Conor stomped his feet and snarled to disperse the Mob, Maja moved on to her next target.

Maja stuck out her imaginary microphone. "And

here's my good buddy, Weez. How's it going, Weez?"

Weez blinked back at her. "Huh? Has practice started?"

"What's wrong, Weez?" Maja sneered. "Did aliens abduct your attention span?"

"No. Just my brother."

Tyler looked at Felix.

"Not worth it," said Felix.

"But Weez is our friend," said Tyler.

"Our friend who doesn't even know when he's been insulted. Five minutes from now, he'll have forgotten that conversation even took place."

Tyler sighed. Felix was right again.

Maja and her Mob moved down the track, trapping Ling-Wa before she could move away. "Attention, Beijing!" Maja shouted to the empty stands. "Put your hands together for Miss Bei Ling-Wa, your teeny, tiny, little hometown hero!"

The Chinese gymnast lifted herself onto her tiptoes and scowled into Maja's smirking face. "I'm not from Beijing, and I'm only a little shorter than you."

"Ouch! That stings!" Maja clutched a hand to her chest. "Yeah, I'm small, but the fans love me anyway. Every time I shred down a mountain, I can feel the crowd giving me a swift kick of energy from behind."

"And I would also like to give you a swift kick in

the behind," said Ling-Wa.

Tyler's hands twitched. He turned to Felix, but the goal-tending giant was no longer by his side. Where had he gone?

Maja wore a sad face, but the corners of her mouth smirked upward. The members of her Mob leaned forward in anticipation, and other players had gathered around as well. "I feel bad for you, Ling-Ling," said Maja. "I've always had a legion of fans, while you grew up performing for brick walls in a gymnastics factory. But then I guess some people just aren't worthy of love and admiration."

Ling-Wa rocked back onto her heels and huffed out all the air from her lungs. She looked even smaller and younger than before, and Tyler's language implant had trouble making out her half-swallowed Mandarin. "I guess not."

If Maja had thrown a punch at Ling-Wa, Tyler could have had her cut from the team. But instead of fists, Maja only used her words. Sharpened words, dipped in poison and delivered to Ling-Wa's weakest spot. And Tyler could only watch, helplessly.

Ling-Wa was an Olympic-level athlete, while Tyler should have been warming a bench on his hometown's soccer team. If a Chinese gymnastics star didn't feel worthy, who was Tyler to tell her otherwise?

Thank god for Felix. He had gathered up Tomoko, Weez, and El Gatito to stand with Ling-Wa and prop her up from behind. Maja might have had her own Mob, but Ling-Wa had something even better: the Challengers.

Only six humans in history had ever taken on an alien team in a Galaxy Games match with interplanetary stakes. One was Tyler. The other five were the players who had helped Tyler take down Stonifer and the Ossmendians in a game that ranged from the Far Side of the Moon to a driveway in Platte Bluff, Nevada.

The Challengers and the Mob faced off in two lines, surrounded by the rest of Team Earth's players. "Raise your hand if you've battled giant stone monsters on the Moon," said Felix. He raised a hand, along with Tomoko, El Gatito, Ling-Wa, and Weez.

Ling-Wa's expression brightened. "Too bad you weren't there, Maja. Your legion of fans would have loved seeing the Ossmendians kick your butt!"

Maja snarled and gnashed her rather large front teeth.

"I've got one," called Colin, from the outside circle of players. A vengeful grin spread across his face. "Raise your hand if you wear a retainer at night in a vain attempt to move your big buck teeth back into place."

"Vikings don't have buck teeth!" Maja shouted, but other players were already pointing, jeering, and making rabbit-faces at her. Maja tried to slink away quietly, but ended up pelted from all sides by crumpled gum wrappers and Frisbees.

The Mob dispersed, and the Challengers retained their undefeated title.

Ling-Wa mouthed a quiet *"danke"* to Felix, a *"gracias"* to El Gatito, an *"arigato"* to Tomoko, and an *"obrigada"* to Weez.

Tyler felt a knot in his stomach. *He* was the team captain. *He* should have been the one to step forward. *He* should have made Maja back down. And if Ling-Wa needed more confidence in herself, *Tyler* should have been the one to give her a pep-talk. Instead, he'd just stood there, frozen, when one of his best players had needed him most.

So much for the legendary Captain Tyler Sato, he thought. As it turned out, Tyler was as useless on the sidelines as he was on the playing field. That hadn't mattered during pre-season training, but it would be a disaster as the hours counted down to the start of the Galaxy Games Tournament.

12

2

NEGZOR COLLECTIVE, PLANET THREE:

Ffargax shifted his shape and became a two-headed frizzlebat. "Where are we going?" he asked through each of the frizzlebat's mouths separately, and then through both at once.

"I can not say," Spawn-Father stated. "And I don't appreciate being harmonized at." The elder Ffifnaxian fixed his eyes straight ahead down the hallway while Ffargax continued flapping around his head.

A Bjarnigast turned the corner ahead and rumbled toward them with its bare claws clicking on the tile floor. Ffargax perched on Spawn-Father's broad shoulder and watched. Had the bulky alien made an odd salute toward Spawn-Father? The same salute as the Dentillian back in the landing bay? And hadn't Spawn-Father returned each of those salutes with his own?

"What was the message that brought us here, Spawn-

Father? This can't be a simple trade mission, like you said. You've never brought me along on a trade mission before." The young shape-shifter became a fuzzy yellow Garm cube and plopped his bulk directly into his spawn-father's path. "I'm not moving until you tell me what's really going on."

"I can not say." Spawn-Father's form, as always, was a massive Cordellian bladderbelt, which plowed Ffargax aside as easily as a drillship plowing through an asteroid.

"You can't say because you don't know?" Ffargax pressed. "Or you can't say because there might be Dwogleys listening in?"

Ffargax had only been teasing, because Spawn-Father took those old myths way too seriously. He wasn't prepared when Spawn-Father turned his angry eyes around and puffed out his bladderbelt throat-sack. "I CAN NOT SAY!" he shouted, with such volume that Ffargax's molecules melted into goo.

Ffargax remained as a shock-puddle for a moment before popping out a reptilian eye and set of mandibles on a stalk. "Why didn't you just say so?"

"Take a proper form," Spawn-Father ordered. "If you mix and match body parts, you'll harden that way. Think of your Great Spawn-Aunt Glynngara."

A ripple passed through Ffargax's puddle form at the thought of Aunt Glynngara, the shame of Planet Ffifnak.

Due to her indecisiveness as a youth, she had hardened as Vremtaxianiod on her left side, and Gormic on the right, and was always at war with herself. Ffargax quickly snapped into the form of a many-tentacled Mrendarian. This way, no matter where Spawn-Father led him, Ffargax would have a slime trail to follow back to safety.

The hallway dead-ended at a huge metal door, guarded by a pair of Zeverians with jagged spikes along the limbs of their black and red exoskeletons. Spawn-Father made his secret gesture and the Zeverians stepped aside.

Ffargax and Spawn-Father passed through the doorway into a downward tunnel that ended in a small circular chamber carved out of granite bedrock. Rings of theater-style seating rose on all sides, scaled to fit a wide variety of galactic beings. Entire sections were enclosed in specialized atmosphere enclosures or water tanks, and each seat featured its own phonic-sphere and flickering holographic interface. "It's like a stadium, but smaller," Ffargax noted. "A theater, perhaps?"*

Spawn-Father nodded almost imperceptibly.

Although hundreds of beings could have fit into the theater, the seats were empty except for one. In a boxed section that jutted out from the rest, an orange macrobe hovered, oval in shape, with a translucent body that allowed Ffargax to see her seatback in a fuzzy outline. Single-celled macrobes were common throughout the galaxy, but this one had a glow unlike any of the clone lines Ffargax had ever seen.

"Seal us in," the macrobe commanded. Organelles pulsed under her membrane, and a field of cilia rippled up and down her body like plant stalks in a strong breeze.

"At once, Supreme Leader," said Spawn-Father.

Ffargax blinked all three of his Mrendarian eyes. In all his life, he'd never seen Spawn Father take orders from anyone.

Thick bladderbelt fingers fumbled over a control console. A metal door slid across the tunnel exit, and every surface in the room buzzed with vibrations. "Causality bubble engaged, Supreme Leader."

"Causality bubble?" asked Ffargax.

"This council chamber now exists outside of space and time," the macrobe explained.

Ffargax popped a nostril-hole with a shrill whistling. "Sounds expensive."

The macrobe's orange glow intensified. "Have a seat, young Ffifnaxian." Her pseudopod indicated the chair to her right in the luxury box.

"My name is Ffargax." He remained on his foot-tentacles in the center of the stage.

"Boy! Do not disobey the Supreme Leader!" Spawn-Father ordered.

"Stand or sit, it matters not." The macrobe's carefree voice was matched by her hypnotic waves of cilia.

"Yes, of course," said Spawn-Father. "The important thing is that he listens."

Ffargax's three eyes boggled at the sight of Spawn-Father conceding an argument. A chill passed down his spinal support column. He climbed into a seat, but made sure it was in a section on the opposite side from the macrobe, with the entire stage between them. "What exactly are you the supreme leader of?" A floating phonic-sphere transmitted his words across the void.

Spawn-Father tensed, but said nothing.

"Ours is an ancient order sworn to protect the galaxy, to defend the Galaxy Games, and to promote galactic civilization. When our ruling council is in session, this chamber holds representatives from a hundred worlds." The Supreme Leader's body varied its glow as she spoke. "An opportunity has arisen for you to join us, young Ffifnaxian."

"Is that so?" asked Ffargax.

"It is," said the Supreme Leader. "Thanks to a helpful informant, we have identified the latest Messenger of the Dwogleys!"

Ffargax closed his three Mrendarian eyes and

steamed out a snicker. "The Messenger? The one and only being in the entire galaxy who can hear the Dwogleys speak? The silliest part of the silliest myth in the history of silly?"

The Supreme Leader slammed her pseudopods on the balcony railing, causing Ffargax to jump back and transform himself into a Tjuffian with a reinforced exoskeleton.

"Mind your words, child," said the macrobe. "You have seen nothing of the galaxy, while I am the 514th daughter-cell in an unbroken line of Supreme Leaders. Do you think yourself a better judge of reality than I am? Do you think my line would waste over five hundred lifetimes hunting a myth?"

"I would hope not," Ffargax admitted.

"In every generation, a Dwogley Messenger pops up somewhere in the galaxy. The Messengers are a tool that those nasty invisible creatures could use to shape the universe of baryonic matter, if we were to allow it. But from the dawn of galactic history, it has been our sacred duty to eliminate each new Messenger by any possible means."

"You eliminate them?" Ffargax laughed. "That almost sounds like you kill them."

"It does sound like that," the Supreme Leader stated.

Ffargax stopped laughing. He noticed Spawn-

Father's muscles tense in his bladderbelt shoulders and limbs. Could he really believe this insanity?

"For an assignment such as this, we need somebody with an advanced language implant—a Galaxy Games player." The Supreme Leader pointed a pseudopod in Ffargax's direction. "It is also helpful for our agent to blend into an alien society and reach the Messenger without being detected. In the past we've had our best luck with young Ffifnaxian shape-shifters, like yourself, who haven't yet hardened into a permanent form."

In the past? Ffargax turned to confront Spawn-Father. "You had an opportunity like this when you were my age, didn't you? There was a Dwogley Messenger they asked you to kill, and—you didn't do it, Spawn-Father, did you?"

"Joining the Order made me the Ffifnaxian I am today," Spawn-Father stated.

Ffargax felt sick to his second spleen. "What if I don't want to be the Ffifnaxian you are today? What if I don't want to be a murderer?"

Spawn-Father hardened his gaze. "Your mission will protect our way of life."

"Your way of life, maybe. The Galaxy Games are my way of life."

"Child," the Supreme Leader spoke softly, "I love the Galaxy Games as much as you. We all do. The games are central to everything we do here at the Order."

Ffargax's thick Tjuffian eyebrows clanked open and shut in surprise. "That seems hard to believe. The games are a celebration of living, not—" He couldn't bring himself to say the words. "Not what you're asking me to do."

The Supreme Leader's glow shifted to a rusty shade, closer to red than orange. "The fondest wish of the Dwogleys is to destroy the Galaxy Games. Without the civilizing influence of the tournament, our entire galaxy would be plunged into never-ending chaos, war, and death!"

Ffargax tried to imagine a galaxy without the games, without challenges between the worlds, and without his own team that advances the interests of Planet Ffifnak. If he couldn't play the game, if he couldn't even watch, what kind of life would he have?

Ffargax looked down at the sharp points on his serrated claws. "How can I save the games?"

The Supreme Leader reached a pseudopod into her body and pulled out a purple crystal. She plugged it into a data port, and a huge spinning hologram appeared in the space above the stage. "This being's name is Tyler Sato. He is the Galaxy Games Captain of Planet Earth, and you must eliminate him any way you can."

"I will," said Ffargax. He thought he saw Spawn-

Father's bladderbelt mouth curve upward at the corners, but that would be impossible. As far as Ffargax had ever known, Spawn-Father never smiled.

3

BEIJING, CHINA:

Tyler had planned several snarky remarks for when Coach Graham finally arrived. *Took you long enough! Did you take a side trip to Mars? Get lost much over the Pacific?* But he had to hold his tongue because when Coach did arrive, he'd brought baklava for the entire team. It's hard to be snarky when someone gives you pastries.

"I found a new coffee shop in Tbilisi." Coach swirled a mug of thick Georgian sludge under Tyler's nose. The fumes burned his eyes and made him choke.

"You used a tigershark for a coffee run?" Tyler asked, with all the snark he could muster.

"I've got to use it while I can. Has the team finished their warm-up drills?"

The pastry-chewing players shuffled guiltily backward, leaving Tyler and Coach alone. "That's not something we've ever done on our own, sir. We usually wait for you."

Coach nodded. "Such a thoughtful boy. I'll always remember that about you." He drained the last drops of coffee, turned his back on Tyler, and headed for the stands.

Tyler exchanged a confused look with Felix and Tomoko. Coach could be flaky, but he'd never walked away from a practice. Tyler expected to blink and find Coach smiling back like always, but no. Coach just kept climbing the stadium steps without a "Just kidding!" or a "Got you!" or even an "April Fools, even though it's June!"

"He'll remember me?" Tyler asked. "Why would he say that?"

"Maybe you've been cut from the team," Tomoko suggested. "Maybe the U.N.'s picked a new captain."

"Maybe it's you," said Tyler.

"Don't even joke about that!"

Except that he hadn't been joking. If anything ever happened to Tyler, his replacement would have to be one of the Challengers. Tomoko and the others had traveled to the Moon and back to defend Earth's slot in the tournament. UNOOSA owed them something for that. Their frequent-flyer miles alone had to be worth a fortune!

Something moved out on the playing field. M'Frozza had popped her purple head out of the metal pyramid and was waving her arm-tentacles to get Tyler's attention. Apparently, the squid-shaped Mrendarian had been inside the metal structure since before the team had arrived.

"I'm going to talk to her," said Tyler. "Maybe she knows what's going on with Coach Graham. Cover for me, Tomoko."

"Who, me?"

"Yeah. Just take charge of the team and lead them through our warm-ups."

Tomoko took a quick series of shallow breaths until she looked like she might pass out. "I can't be responsible for all that!"

"Fine." Tyler looked over the rest of his team and rested his eyes on Felix. Strong, reliable, dependable Felix. If Tomoko wouldn't step up, the big German surely would. "*You're* in charge," he said, with a nod in Felix's direction.

But a boy in a blue leather cat mask jumped out from behind Felix, pumped his arm, and shouted, "Finally!" The Mexican *luchador* jumped forward and gave Tyler a sharp salute. "Do not worry, Captain Tyler. El Gatito will whip this team into shape!"

"But—I didn't mean—" Tyler looked back over at

Felix, who returned his gaze with a wince and a shrug. "Okay, fine," said Tyler. If anything bad happened with the cat-eared wrestler in charge, at least that would bring Coach Graham down from the stands. Tyler hustled out to see M'Frozza before anyone could try to change his mind.

M'Frozza was a Galaxy Games captain like Tyler, but not really like Tyler, because M'Frozza wasn't a fake. She really was an interstellar athlete, trained to lead since the day she was . . . born? Hatched? Cloned? Tyler frowned. He had no idea how Mrendarian children came to exist, and there didn't seem to be an appropriate way to ask.

"Greetings, Captain Tyler," M'Frozza burbled cheerfully. "Technician N'Gatu is just now completing the installation, so *wink and thumbs-up!*" She closed her middle eye and flicked one of her arm-tentacles, splattering mustardy slime directly into Tyler's face.

Tyler wiped the alien goop from his eyes. "It's nice that you're trying to pick up a few human-type gestures. But for a proper thumbs-up, you need at least one thumb."

"Imagine I have a thumb," said the squid-shaped girl. "Then imagine it's way, way up!"

Tyler shook his head. "I wish I felt as good about things as you do, M'Frozza. This is our last day of practice. Tomorrow we're leaving Earth. Then the tournament begins, with real games that really matter and everybody watching."

"*Shoulder shrug,*" M'Frozza replied. Two of her arm-tentacles sprayed slime in all directions. This time, Tyler dodged out of the way. "Your team has been training hard, and they look good to me."

They glanced over at the track, where El Gatito stood on one foot with his hands curved into claws above his head. "Make yourself look big! Make yourself look big! And hiss, and hiss, and now the other foot!" The players mirrored the *luchador*'s movements like a pack of history's most embarrassed cats.

"See? They look . . . good," said M'Frozza.

Tyler stared at her.

"Really," said M'Frozza. "Your players may have their quirks, but they are all highly skilled. They will do fine in the tournament."

"They'd do better with a real leader," said Tyler. "Is it too late to change captains?"

"*Raise eyebrows!*" M'Frozza declared. Her middle eye twitched slightly.

"You don't have eyebrows," Tyler told her.

"Imagine that I do, and that I have just raised them in surprise. You, Captain Tyler, are a planetary champion. You have won challenges. No one else is qualified to be Earth's captain."

Tyler lowered his voice to a whisper. "But you know I'm not *really* a champion. I only won our challenge game because you let me win, and I would never have beaten Stonifer if Daiki hadn't knocked my shot into the hoop. Earth's only real hope in these games is if they replace me with someone who isn't me. Anyone who isn't me."

He and M'Frozza looked back at the team again. El Gatito was now flexing his skinny arms like a bodybuilder. "You will be like El Gatito, yes? El Gatito is fierce! El Gatito is strong! El Gatito is someone you don't want to mess with!"

"*Almost* anyone who isn't me," Tyler corrected.

"Friend Tyler, your team would follow you into the heart of a supernova. You lack only the self-confidence to lead them, but that is why we are here today." M'Frozza shook out her face-tentacles and turned toward the metal pyramid. "Technician N'Gatu!"

The pyramid remained silent, except for a steady drip-drip-drip from the rusty pipes.

"Technician N'Gatu!" M'Frozza called again.

"Maybe he's up in the stands with a mug of alien coffee," said Tyler. "Because why should Mrendarian adults be any more reliable than human adults?"

"Technician N'Gatu!" M'Frozza's whistle-shrill tone

felt like an icepick through Tyler's skull.

From the bottom of the pyramid, a Mrendarian head popped through an impossibly tiny hole. This was followed by half a dozen arm-tentacles, though most of N'Gatu's body remained inside. "What? Who? Me?" Beads of yellow slime rolled down the technician's face.

"We've been calling you," said Tyler. "Is something wrong?"

"Of course not!" The technician rubbed an arm-tentacle across his slimy forehead. "And if there were something wrong, it certainly would not be *my* fault."

"Okay." Tyler didn't know what else to say so he just nodded.

"Technician, we are ready for you to activate the obstacle system," said M'Frozza.

"I haven't received authorization from—"

"Now, Technician, now!" M'Frozza shouted.

"Very well. If you will excuse me, Captains." N'Gatu squeezed back inside, leaving a ring of slime on the edge of his access hole. When he spoke again, his voice was muffled by the metal walls. "I suggest you clear the area. With haste."

The pipes belched smoke in alternating puffs of pink, purple, and red, as an earthquake rumbled the ground. Tyler knew from the schematic that the little pyramid was like the tip of an iceberg, while the main part of the mechanism stretched underground from sideline to sideline.

"Clearing the area!" Tyler took off at an arms-flailing run. M'Frozza slid across the grass beside him. Both planetary captains struggled as the turf puckered and rippled all around them.

At the edge of the field, they found the other Earth players curled up on the ground. Tyler nudged El Gatito with his foot.

"The Power-Nap of Deep Meditation is not done yet," El Gatito mumbled. He stretched and yawned, just like a cat. "Come back in about fifteen—what?" The whiskers on his mask bounced as he sat up. N'Gatu's pyramid puffed out a mushroom cloud of green, yellow, and blue, and the entire stadium roared like a beehive that had fallen into a blender that had fallen into a trash compactor.

Earth players jumped in surprise. Maja's goggles flew off her face. Weez shouted his brother's name. Others achieved a new personal best in the vertical leap, but one player jumped higher than the rest. Baashi, the Somali cricket star, arched his back, pumped his arms and legs, and landed with a mad scramble onto the field. "Take cover in the fog! The enemy won't see us there—or so I've heard!"

"That's not a fog bank!" Tyler shouted, but Baashi had already vanished into the colorful wall of smoke.

"Oh, this is perfect!" M'Frozza gleefully burbled.

Weez grabbed a handful of M'Frozza's arm-tentacles and spun her around. "What's going on? Is Baashi being abducted? He is, isn't he?" Weez let go of M'Frozza and ran to the edge of the field of churning grass. "Hey, Baashi! Ask them if they've seen my brother!"

"Nobody's being abducted," said Tyler. Or at least, he didn't think so.

The smoke thinned enough that the Somali boy could be seen running circles, flapping his arms, and screaming. Tyler checked the stands to see if this, at least, would bring Coach Graham down to the field, but no. Coach checked his watch and continued nursing his coffee.

The pyramid's rumbling dropped to a dull whir, which only made Baashi's terrified screams sound even louder.

"N'Gatu must have seen that Baashi was on the field. Good. Now we can get him out of there." Tyler took a step forward, but M'Frozza stopped him with one arm-tentacle stretched out in classic crossing-guard style.

"Not yet," she stated.

Tyler gave her a quizzical look.

"Oh, how I envy your eyebrows," M'Frozza exclaimed. "You can raise them so high!"

"Thanks. And I envy your—" Tyler looked at her slime-coated purple skin, three big golden eyes, and masses of squirming tentacles. "Personality."

On the field, Baashi had dropped, whimpering, to his knees. For a former child-soldier, he sure wasn't the fearless warrior Tyler had thought he was getting.

"The longer we let him freak out, the longer it'll take to calm him down," said Tyler.

"You must wait," M'Frozza insisted. "Or do you mistrust me?"

Tyler narrowed his eyes. "You lie. You keep secrets. You manipulate people. I'd like to trust you, M'Frozza, but you sure don't make it easy."

"We keep each other's secrets," M'Frozza reminded him, as if he had another choice.

Tyler turned back to watch Baashi blink back his tears and take a bracing breath. The Somali boy brushed the dirt off his practice uniform and laughed out loud. "I am unharmed! This is just like arriving at a battle to find the enemy has already surrendered— or so I've heard."

The other players cheered. Baashi danced with joy. Up in the stands, Coach Graham spoke into his mobile phone. And back on the sideline, M'Frozza counted down to herself.

"Three . . . two . . . one . . . ."

Suddenly, the turf all around Baashi burst open with a thousand tiny explosions. Spinning rotors and giant claws popped out of the ground, along with tower-mounted water cannons and a maze of moving walls. The obstacle course looked like a factory-themed amusement park ride, spread over an entire soccer field.

Clumps of dirt and turf rained down on the rest of the team. "Great," said Felix. "There goes our security deposit on the stadium."

"Baashi, get out of there!" Tyler urged.

Baashi zigged and zagged, but the obstacle system kept tossing new barriers and challenges directly in his path. He ducked under a curtain of knives, side-stepped a pit of snakes, and stumbled onto a conveyor belt that zipped him into a pool of mud. While the entire team shouted for Baashi to get up, he curled himself into a trembling ball.

"There." M'Frozza slapped an arm-tentacle against Tyler's back. "*Now* you may go out there and get him."

4

CAMP GALAXY, SASKATCHEWAN, CANADA:

In the form of a Hidranian swamp worm, Ffargax slithered through the grass at the edge of the human encampment. He used a miniature energy cannon on its lowest setting to overload one of the security cameras. If the mission planners at the Order had calculated correctly, this should have created a flickering blind spot in the camp's defenses. It would last for just a few pulses, and if the humans noticed it at all, it would look like a malfunctioning diode.

Ffargax flowed through a gap in the electrified fence. A human patrol passed by, consisting of five peacekeepers whose woodland camouflage uniforms were betrayed by flat cloth hats in a shockingly bright shade of turquoise blue. All of them failed to see Ffargax blended into the grass. Once they were gone, the shape-shifter took the form of a human adult, blending the features he had seen, and choosing pale skin and medium brown hair. He completed the disguise by forming his outer skin into fatigues, combat boots, and the signature blue beret. The energy cannon hung off his belt like a shiny brass key, but otherwise he looked just like any of the others. On his way to the cluster of player cabins, a group of genuine peacekeepers even waved to him.

Ffargax found the cabins empty. A group of human adults stood nearby with a collection of bags and suitcases. They drank hot fluids and talked. Ffargax pretended to take a sentry position while he listened in. They spoke several different languages, but some spoke more than one language, so there could be something of a conversation among them. Ffargax's language implant really was handy for spy work, just as the Supreme Leader had predicted.

The adults turned out to be the family members of several players on the team. They had been taking turns as team chaperones for seven-day intervals, and the current shift was coming to an end. The next group would be the ones to join the Earth team for their tournament's opening round, becoming the first human beings to ever leave their own solar system.

Ffargax remembered everyone's excitement at the news of a primitive culture claiming a spot in the upcoming tournament. The analysts all crowed about *how the Galaxy Games provided equal opportunity for all planets in the Galaxy. But over time, questions had been raised. Like why had Tyler challenged M'Frozza behind the closed doors of a Mrendarian shuttle, orbiting high above Planet Earth? And why had Tyler and Stonifer started their game on Earth's uninhabited moon, completely hidden from spectators?*

If the Supreme Leader was right, and Earth's challenges really had been manipulated by Dwogleys, the team's captain would have to be stopped before he corrupted the entire tournament.

The arriving chaperones dragged their suitcases into the cabins. The others started down the path to the departure buses. It could be a while before Tyler Sato arrived, so Ffargax took the form of a native pine tree to wait.

As the old Ffifnaxian proverb said, time flies when you're imitating vegetation.

5

BEIJING, CHINA:

Tyler stared at M'Frozza. "Why wouldn't you let me grab Baashi *before* this field became a mechanical deathtrap?"

"*Wry knowing grin!*" M'Frozza wriggled her face-tentacles.

El Gatito wedged himself between the two planetary captains and placed his hands on his hips. "Somebody needs to save the day. Somebody bold. Somebody heroic. Somebody with cat ears and a bright red cape!"

"Wait!" Tyler shouted, as the cat-boy leapt onto the field. Inches away from the spot where El Gatito's foot touched the turf, a six-foot jet of flame shot out of the ground.

El Gatito jumped back across the sideline, and patted out a small fire on the corner of his cape. "On second thought, feel free to start without me."

After that, nobody else seemed eager to risk their lives on the obstacle field. Hari, the one kid who lived for bouncing off walls and scrambling over obstacles, stood poised and wriggling with nervous energy. But even he wasn't eager to tackle a mechanical killing field.

"Shouldn't Coach Graham step in here? He's the adult in charge, supposedly." Tyler looked to the stands, but Coach was no longer there. Overhead, a tigershark ascended into the night. "He's leaving! Right in the middle of a practice! Right in the middle of an *emergency*!"

"*Puffed-out breath of exasperation!*" M'Frozza exclaimed, and puffs of steam really did pop out of her nostril-holes. "You can do this, Captain Tyler. The obstacle system is designed to challenge ordinary players, but any real Galaxy Games captain can navigate the field without difficulty."

Tyler gazed out at the field and imagined himself facing some random obstacle. Something easy. Like, for example, a narrow rope bridge. He placed an Imaginary Tyler at the start of the bridge and watched him go.

Imaginary Tyler gripped the railing.

Imaginary Tyler took a few steps.

Imaginary Tyler turned.

Imaginary Tyler smiled.

Imaginary Tyler waved.

Imaginary Tyler got sliced in half as a massive pendulum blade swept across the bridge.

Tyler winced. "No difficulty, huh? Maybe I should wear a blindfold to make it a challenge."

Nearby, Maja grabbed her invisible microphone and rocked her sportscaster voice. "Attention, sports fans! The Great and Powerful Tyler Sato, Planetary Captain, Lunar Explorer, Slayer of Stone-Boys, and Tamer of Squid-Girls will now rescue Baashi from a mechanical deathtrap *while blindfolded!*"

Maja's Mob gathered around her.

Tyler blinked. "I didn't actually mean I would—"

Valya enfolded Tyler in a hug that actually felt pretty nice, for a last-ever embrace. "It is such a brave thing you do!" By the end of the hug, and kisses on both cheeks, the entire team had gathered.

Hari stepped forward with a strip of white cloth, possibly the very one that had gotten him into the record books for most blindfolded backflips in under ten minutes. "You may wear this," Hari said, and before Tyler could protest, the cloth was wrapped tightly over his eyes.

Someone spun Tyler around like he was about to

pin the tail on a donkey. Someone else pushed him toward the sound of whirring, buzzing, whooshing—and way off in the distance, Baashi's whimpering voice.

Someone else put a hand on his shoulder and asked, in German, "What are you doing?"

Tyler took a centering breath. His guts were screaming in protest, but he'd gotten really good at projecting calmness and playing the role of Great and Powerful Tyler Sato, Planetary Captain, Lunar Explorer, Slayer of Stone-Boys, and Tamer of Squid-Girls. "I'm going to save Baashi, I guess. I mean, somebody has to, right? And like you said, I'm the only authority figure around."

"Okay sure, but blindfolded? This is madness!"

"Madness would be taking the blindfold off," said Tyler. Because if he had to actually look at all those alien death machines again, he'd end up whimpering and helpless just like Baashi.

"You can't let Maja back you into a corner," said Felix. "This brave front is going to get you killed. Let someone else take care of this. There's me and Ling, and Tomoko, and Weez, and El Gatito...."

Tyler felt his eyebrows rub against the inside of the blindfold as he frowned. "I know you mean well, Felix, but the Challengers can't keep fighting all my battles."

He heard Felix sigh. "Please, Tyler. If you die, the

team dies with you. We won't be able to go on."

"Of course you will." Tyler shrugged his shoulder from Felix's hand and took a single step forward. Then another. Then another. His right sneaker found the edge of a ridge of turf that was just high enough to guide his steps. Another ridge on his left side pushed him over in time to avoid something that clanged like a snapping bear trap.

The players behind him shouted, "To your left! To your left! No, your *other* left!"

Tyler sidestepped a blast of hot air that might have been a jet of flame. The ground sloped steeply upward but the ridge guidelines continued, curving like a mountain path that twisted and turned back on itself. Tyler found a railing and climbed as quickly as he could.

"You're at the top! Now reach for the zip-line!" called Conor. In a quieter voice he added, "It's a good thing he can't see all those mechanical alligators."

"Mechanical alligators?" Tyler felt his heart double-beat. "And what was that about a zip-line?" Tyler stood on tip-toes and stretched his hands upward. His fingers only just brushed against a bar that clattered from a chain above.

He had to jump to grab onto it with both hands. The wind that rushed by his ears didn't quite cover the sound of snapping and gnashing from below. "Mechanical alligators. Why does it always have to be mechanical alligators?"

The bar yanked out of Tyler's hands. He spent a panicked moment in free-fall before landing butt-first on a rubbery surface that bounced him back into the air. After two more bounces, he came down was on a surface that felt like an overstuffed gym mat.

"Right onto the revolving platform?" Maja demanded. "How lucky can you get?"

"It's not luck," said Hari. "Tyler Sato is the greatest athlete in the history of the world!"

Tyler could almost hear Maja rolling her eyes. Under the blindfold, his own eyes were rolling. Tyler moved forward, feeling with his hands until he found the edge of the platform. When he tried to stand, the spinning motion of the ground made his stomach churn. He could hear Baashi's whimpering get louder, then softer, then louder again, now with a few broken-up words in Somali that his language implant couldn't quite work out.

"He'll never be able to time his jump to hit the ice bridge," said Maja. "Especially with that blindfold on."

"But Tyler Sato is the greatest athlete in the history of the world!" at least five kids said at once, and Hari shouted, "Go, Tyler!"

"You're officially out of the Mob," Maja snapped.

Tyler stood on wobbly legs, holding his arms out for balance. He felt for the platform edge with his foot while listening hard. If the ice bridge was in Baashi's direction, Tyler would have to jump at the moment when Baashi's voice was at its loudest. Or maybe a second before. Not that he was an expert at timing jumps, but he'd picked up a few tips from moving Mario and Luigi around a video game landscape.

Tyler waited through another cycle, timed the jump in his mind, and pushed off.

In the air, a strange thought came to him. Tyler had spent every day of the past two years waiting for the one misplaced step that would turn him from World's Most Celebrated Athlete to World's Most Laughed-At Failure. That step was long overdue. And now, here he was at last with an absolutely certain chance of failing spectacularly in front of his entire team. Then somebody else would have to save Baashi and Tyler both. That somebody would probably become the new team captain, and lead the team onward to alien worlds. Meanwhile, Tyler would go home to watch the Galaxy Games on TV with his disappointed family.

He would probably be too embarrassed to ever leave the house.

Tyler's sneakers came down on a surface that was

hard, slippery, and downward sloping. The ice seemed to move beneath his feet, pushing him this way and that. Tyler's Falcon Zero-Weights had retractable spikes that could have given them a biting grip on the ice, but only if he activated them with a precise heel-click. Tyler shifted his feet, desperately brought the sneakers together, and even shouted, "There's no place like home!" like Dorothy in *The Wizard of Oz*.

It didn't work.

Instead, Tyler shot forward so fast, it felt like he'd been fired out of a cannon.

"Insane! He's going for the ski-jump!" Maja exclaimed. "Without skis!"

"Ski jump?" Tyler barely had time to process those words before the ice curved upward under his sneakers and he completely lost track of gravity.

Tyler tumbled and floated. Falling while blindfolded was so peaceful, Tyler almost forgot it could end with an iron spike, a pool of acid, or worse. Instead, his sneakers came down into a squooshy mass that swallowed his feet up to his calves.

"A triple-double and he sticks the landing!" Ling-Wa proclaimed.

The other kids burst into cheers.

"Sure, but how hard is it to stick a landing in twenty centimeters of mud?" asked Maja.

"Tyler Sato is incredible," Valya gushed.

"You're out of the Mob too!" Maja snapped.

When Tyler's heart stopped hammering so loudly in his chest, he could hear Baashi's voice next to his feet. This close, Tyler could finally pick out the softly mumbled words. "I'm sorry, Commander. The failure is all mine. Punish me, but spare my village."

"It's okay, Baashi," said Tyler.

"I don't want to fight," said Baashi. "Please, Commander, don't send me on another raid."

Tyler removed his blindfold and saw the boy rolling in the same pit of mud he had landed in. Machinery whirled and clashed all around them. "You're not in the militia anymore, Baashi. You're a Galaxy Games player now."

"It was an ambush, Commander. No one else survived."

Tyler didn't know exactly what the boy had gone through, but it was painful to even watch him act it out. "Snap out of it, Baashi. You're safe now." A salvo of spike-covered spheres flew through the rainbow haze over their heads. "Almost safe," Tyler corrected. He shook Baashi by the shoulders, but that only made the boy shriek louder.

Tyler could only think of one way to break Baashi out of his funk. It seemed cruel, but he had to get him back on his feet. "Private Baashi!" he shouted. "You are a disgrace to that uniform! Fall into formation on the double!"

"Sir, yes, sir!" Baashi jumped up and stood at attention. Mud dripped from his face and clothing. The Somali boy blinked several times and surveyed his surroundings. "Captain Tyler?"

"You're safe now," Tyler told him.

All around them, the obstacle system ground to a halt. The walls and ramps melted away, the spinning rotors retracted back into the ground, and the mud pit sprouted a fresh coating of grass. Within seconds, the field looked exactly as it had when the team first arrived.

"Thanks, N'Gatu!" Tyler called out to the control pyramid, which stood just a few feet away.

One of the Mrendarian technician's three eyes peeked out through a triangle-shaped flap at the point. "Don't thank me yet, Captain Tyler. You have no idea of the ancient vendetta I've called down on your head. I'm so sorry!"

"What are you talking about?" Tyler asked. "What ancient vendetta?"

"Yeep! You weren't supposed to hear that! Pretend I said nothing. Nothing at all!" The flap slammed shut, and the pyramid went silent except for a steady drip-

drip-drip from the pipes.

The Earth players stormed onto the field, stepping cautiously, to make sure Baashi was all right and to offer Tyler an assortment of high-fives, fist-bumps, and backslaps. Fortuna, the team's part-time windsurfer and full-time Caribbean psychic, thanked the spirit world for protecting her captain.

Bader waved a smartphone that he technically wasn't allowed to carry around. "I got the whole thing on video, and it's going viral!"

"Of course it is." Tyler sighed. "I can't take a *nap* without going viral."

"You're out of the Mob, you're out of the Mob, and you're out of the Mob," said Maja, dismissing her three remaining followers. "And as for you—" She pointed a finger at Tyler's nose. "—that was actually pretty cool. Not Viking-cool but still, not bad for an American cowboy."

Tyler shrugged. He was certainly no cowboy, but that was the best compliment he would ever get out of Maja.

After making sure the other players were giving Baashi the space he needed, Tyler stomped over to M'Frozza. Her face-tentacles radiated smugness. "Nice rescue, Captain Tyler."

"You knew I'd be all right," Tyler accused her.

"Of course."

"How?"

"It is just as I told you. The obstacle system is designed to challenge ordinary players, but any real Galaxy Games captain can navigate the field without any trouble at all. It's all in the programming—but that's our secret, even from your UNOOSA. Especially from your UNOOSA."

"Why would you do this to me?"

"After today, none can ever challenge your qualifications. None can claim to match you. None can replace you." She leaned forward, assaulting Tyler's senses with the mustard tang of her slime. "And therefore, you cannot quit."

"So the whole purpose of that gigantic machine was to keep me from quitting the team?"

"I suspected you might try."

"And I was never in any danger?"

M'Frozza tapped an arm-tentacle against the side of her head. "You believed your life was at risk but you stepped onto the course anyway, in order to help a teammate. That makes you a worthy captain."

Tyler dropped down, cross-legged, onto the grass. No matter what they said in *The Hunger Games*, having the odds stacked ever in your favor was a terrible thing. It didn't matter that he hadn't known about it. It didn't matter that he hadn't asked for it. It still made him a cheater. Again. "Thanks for nothing, M'Frozza. If you were a *real* friend, you'd have let me quit the team. Instead, you've just set me up for an even bigger failure on an even bigger stage."

The squid-girl looked away. "Your bravery has earned you a place in the tournament, as surely as my cowardice has earned me a place in the stands."

Whatever that meant.

Tyler lay back in the grass. The nerves in his arms and legs still tingled from the adrenaline in his bloodstream. "This practice is a loss. Let's go back to Camp Galaxy. Safe, dull, boring old Camp Galaxy, where nothing exciting or dangerous ever happens."

6

CAMP GALAXY, SASKATCHEWAN, CANADA:

The Earth team summer headquarters sprawled across ten thousand acres of wooded lakefront, deep in the Canadian wilderness, isolated from world politics—and especially from the growing Seclusionist movement, which sought to protect humanity from alien influences by pulling Earth out of the Galaxy Games.

Maps referred to the plot as UNOOSA Property 7, but most people just called it Camp Galaxy, featuring unpaved trails, outdoor bathrooms, lots of mosquitoes, wooden cabins, constant athletic drills, a fleet of spaceships, a squadron of U.N. peacekeepers, a geodesic dome for alien visitors, and an international-themed restaurant.

The three tigersharks returned to camp at ten in the morning, local time, just minutes after leaving

Beijing. The doors yawned open with the hiss of ten thousand soda cans and, one at a time, thirty-six of Earth's greatest young athletes stepped out.

Plus a very tired Tyler Sato.

Miss Wen met the team at the landing lot, waving a clipboard of pages covered in neat hand-printed Roman script with Vietnamese accent marks. It might have been Tyler's imagination, but her tight bun of black hair looked frazzled at the edges, and her thick-rimmed glasses seemed to have slid a half-inch farther down her narrow nose. "Welcome back, Mr. Sato. You're two hours early, but I suppose that's to be expected, given the events of the day."

Tyler looked around at the other players. He'd hoped the video of his blindfolded obstacle run hadn't reached UNOOSA, but as fast as the tigersharks were, the Internet was even faster.

The administrator's lips puckered into a lemon-sour expression. "Image control is vital for the success of your team, Mr. Sato. Especially right now. Influential voices were already saying it's too dangerous to send twelve- and thirteen-year-olds into space—and you've just handed them a video filled with laser blasts and acid streams."

"Wait," said Tyler. "There were laser blasts and acid streams?"

"A few," Felix told him.

Wen sighed. "At least you gave the new obstacle system a good trial run."

"It did exactly what it was designed to do," Tyler told her, truthfully.

"I would certainly hope so, considering how obscenely much it cost."

"Miss Wen?" Tomoko asked. "Since practice was so crazy and ended so early, and since I have a new volume of Hunter-Elf Zeita manga to read, can we please have some free time?"

"An excellent question, Miss Tomizawa. According to your coaching notes—" Wen frowned at the page on her clipboard, then flipped it over dismissively. "But of course, that no longer applies. Let's say free time until lunch, then an afternoon drill, followed by dinner and a good night's sleep. That last part is vital, so no forlorn watching of the skies all night and into the morning hours." She looked pointedly at Weez.

"Even if I can't get to sleep?" Weez asked.

"Dr. Luchenkov will administer whatever sleep aids are necessary." Miss Wen flipped another page, clicked her ballpoint pen, and made a quick note. "You will awaken fresh and well-rested tomorrow morning, ready for a full itinerary of Departure Day events and your interstellar flight to the Arena District on Planet

Shpill. Those events are as follows . . ."

Tyler was amazed at how Miss Wen's voice remained calm, even as she described the parades, parties, and celebrations of Departure Day, the most elaborate media event in history, leading up to the first-ever trip by humans to an alien world.

After years of training, his team would be going into space, where no one had gone before.

"Any questions?" Miss Wen asked.

"Oh, oh, oh!" El Gatito waved his hand in the air.

Miss Wen sighed. "Yes, Mr. Gatito?"

"Will there be ice cream? El Gatito loves ice cream!"

Miss Wen made herself another note. "I will put in a request. Consider yourselves dismissed until lunch."

The players cheered. A few planned to call home during their free time, or to meet up with the newly-arrived family members who would chaperone the team into space. Tyler's dad was supposed to be among them, but Miss Wen said his tigershark had not yet arrived.

"I've got to find Daiki-san," said Tomoko. "I promised not to break into the new manga without him, and this might be our last chance for a while."

Tyler shrugged. "Cousin Daiki's been spending all his free time in the woods on some kind of secret project. I think he's planning some new tricks with the camera drone, so good luck finding him."

"I could consult the spirits for you," Fortuna offered, as she took a pouch of charcoal dust from her pocket.

"Consulting the spirits is your answer for everything," said Maja. "Why do you have to be so weird?"

"An excellent question!" Fortuna tossed a pinch of dust into the air. "I'll consult the spirits on that as well."

Weez claimed dibs on the media room, and Felix organized a pick-up game of soccer, but before the team could disperse, a flock of Canada geese scattered as a fourth tigershark dropped out of the sky. Tyler recognized the distinctive markings of Coach Graham's shark painted on the side.

"So nice of Coach to join us," said Tyler. "I hope he's enjoying his fresh mug of Columbian fair-trade dark roast, or whatever was more important to him than our safety."

Felix stepped between Tyler and the tigershark with all the speed of a premiere goalie. "Tyler, please don't start anything you'll be sorry for later."

"I'm not the one who started anything!" Tyler shouted. "It was Coach Graham who walked out on our practice."

"He must have had a reason. And he did bring us pastries."

"Is that all our lives are worth? A big bag of baklava?" Tyler looked around at his suddenly quiet teammates.

"It was very good baklava," El Gatito ventured. The others nodded and licked their lips.

"He's our coach, Tyler," said Felix. "Even you have to respect that."

Tyler sighed. "Felix, you're a good friend. You have a big heart, and I don't know anyone who's even half as forgiving as you are."

A blush colored Felix's puffy cheeks. "Thanks!"

"But I'm not you. Now get out of my way!"

Felix raised his arms in surrender, and Tyler marched past him toward Coach's tigershark. Other players crowded in to back Tyler up in what was sure to be an epic confrontation. The angry words looping in Tyler's head had been building for months, and what was the worst Coach could do? Cut Tyler from the team? After the stunt M'Frozza had pulled with the obstacle system, Tyler probably couldn't be fired for anything less than stealing a tigershark, crashing it into an alien stadium, and stumbling out in his underwear!

The first syllable was already forming in Tyler's mouth as the tigershark door dropped open, but the only noise that came out was a confused "*Bluh?*"

Standing in the jaws of the tigershark was a tall, powerfully-built man with oversized gold rings and enormous diamond-stud earrings. Tyler took three steps back, which was only possible because the players behind him had shuffled backward as well.

"That's not Coach Graham," stated El Gatito. "Not unless Coach grew ten centimeters taller. And shaved his head. And grew a pair of bushy eyebrows. And got some shoulder implants. And darkened his skin. And put on sparkly jewelry. And started wearing snazzy light-colored suits."

"We can all see that it's not him!" Tomoko snapped.

"Unless he was abducted by aliens who altered his appearance," said Weez. The other players grumbled and scoffed. "Really, I'll bet that happens a lot!"

Tyler swallowed hard. "What is Auggie Lang doing here?"

Fortuna tapped one of her hearing aids like she thought her language implant might have gone faulty. "What's an Auggie Lang?"

Tyler stared at her. It seemed crazy that anyone could fail to recognize Auggie "Leadbelly" Lang, but other players seemed equally confused. Didn't anyone outside the United States follow the NFL? "He was a football coach—American football, not soccer football.

Auggie Lang took four different teams to the Super Bowl. He's a legend! But he retired a few seasons back, so why is he here? And why is he riding in Coach Graham's tigershark?"

"Maybe he's covering for Coach Graham," said Tomoko.

"Maybe he ate Coach Graham for breakfast," said El Gatito.

Mr. Lang glared down at the team, forcing each player to turn away from his gaze. His voice seemed to shake the trees. "My name is Auggie Lang. I will be replacing Coach Graham. For the duration of the tournament, I will be in charge of your strength training, conditioning, and ongoing motivation."

"Motivation?" asked Maja.

Lang made a fist and cracked each of his knuckles with a loud pop. "Motivation is my specialty. I've been known to motivate a team out of the league's basement, up a dozen flights of stairs, and into the penthouse suite."

Tyler imagined climbing a spiral staircase that wrapped around the entire galaxy. It made him dizzy just thinking about it, but Lang did have a reputation for getting results. He also had a reputation for punching through lockers, doors, and walls when he got angry.

The other players looked frightened and confused by their new coach, and even Fortuna's mouth hung open in an expression of surprise that Tyler had never seen on the self-proclaimed psychic.

"What happened to Coach Graham?" asked Felix. "Is he sick?"

"I have it right here!" Bader waved his phone and pointed at the screen. "All the top headlines are about Coach Graham, and no wonder he was so distracted at practice. A Seclusionist group kidnapped his family, and forced him to quit the team!"

A hushed murmur spread through the team, and Tyler felt awful for thinking Coach Graham only cared about his coffee. The Seclusionists were bad news. They wanted to keep Earth isolated from alien influences, including the Galaxy Games. *Especially* the Galaxy Games. Over the past two years, as Departure Day approached, the Seclusionist groups had grown more numerous, more vocal, and more desperate—but still, Tyler never would have thought they'd target anyone's family.

"We still have all our assistant coaches, don't we?" Tyler asked. "Coach Singh? Coach Batista?"

Bader shook his head. "They were scared off too. What a disaster!"

"I need to call my father and brother to make sure

they're all right," said Felix. "Bader, hand over that phone!"

"And I need to check on *Obaa-chan*," said Tomoko. "If the Seclusionists attacked her, she might have hurt them!"

Tyler wanted to call his own parents and his sister, but Bader and his phone had already vanished under a pile of desperate players.

Lang cleared his throat, and everybody froze in place. He put out his hand, palm up, and shot Bader the same glare that made grown NFL linebackers hang their heads in shame. Apparently, it also worked on golf prodigies, because Bader silently stepped forward and dropped his phone into Auggie Lang's palm.

"Um, Mr. Lang?" Tyler's voice cracked and squeaked like a mouse.

Lang narrowed his eyes at the Earth team's captain. A tiny twitch of the coach's right eyebrow granted permission to speak.

"We lost Coach Graham when the Seclusionists threatened his family. How do we know that won't happen with you?"

Lang frowned. "No need to worry. I don't have a family."

"No parents? No wife? No children?" asked El Gatito. "Brothers? Sisters? Third cousins?"

"I grew up fine without a family, and I don't need one now. As for children, they didn't impress me even when I was one of them."

Tyler frowned. If Lang hated kids so much, how was he going to be their coach?

"We'll start slow," Lang promised the team. "I have three simple questions, and if you answer correctly, you may have a slice of chocolate cake. Children like cake, don't they? I think I read that somewhere." The coach's forced grin somehow looked even scarier than his scowl.

"Are these questions multiple choice?" asked El Gatito.

Lang fixed his gaze with laser intensity. "First question! Who are you?"

El Gatito faltered. "*Señior*, I am a *luchador*. My true identity is a carefully-guarded secret, hidden behind the mask of the *luchador*." He tapped the blue leather cat mask that wrapped around his head. "But the masses call me El Gatito Grande."

"The Great Kitten," Lang noted. "*¡Excellente!*"

"*Gracias*," said El Gatito, obviously pleased with himself. "What is your second question?"

Lang narrowed his eyes. "What do you want?"

"What I want is to know your second question."

"Let's not make this a comedy routine," said Lang.

"What do you want, Kitten?"

"I want to fight!" El Gatito made his hands into claws and hissed like a cat. "These questions are too easy. Bring on number three!"

"Where are you from?" Lang asked.

"Mexico City," said El Gatito.

Lang's expression darkened. "Wrong answer!" His shout made the entire team jump. "Take ten laps around the landing area!"

"But I'm not wrong," said El Gatito in confusion.

"Ten laps, Kitten!"

El Gatito set off at a run.

"You!" Lang pointed an accusing finger at Weez. "Who are you?"

"Luiz Rafael Vila Lobos," said Weez.

Lang blinked back at him.

"Everyone calls me Weez for short, ever since my little brother couldn't pronounce my real name when he was just a baby."

"What a heartwarming story," said Lang. "It must have been nice that you and your brother were so close."

"It was, until he got abducted by aliens."

Lang rubbed a tired finger under his eyes and along the bridge of his nose. "What do you want, Weez-for-short?"

"To find my brother."

Lang's bushy eyebrows inched upward.

"And also to be the best ever at *futebol*," Weez added quickly. "Which is why I'm on the team. That's the answer you were looking for, yes?" He looked up at Lang for a long and awkward moment.

"Where are you from, Weez-for-short?"

Weez grinned. "That's easy! Brazil."

"Wrong answer!" Lang bellowed. "Take ten laps!"

Again and again and again, Lang asked his three questions. The first two usually went well, but the third question always turned out to be wrong. Absolutely wrong. Wrong enough to cause a bout of red-faced screaming and a demand for ten laps.

"The cake is a lie," Maja grumbled, as she became the latest player to begin a jog around the landing lot. After her, Fortuna was the last in line, aside from Tyler.

As Lang approached, Fortuna tapped and adjusted her hearing aids.

Lang bent down and leaned forward into her face. "Am I not coming through clearly enough for you?"

Fortuna shook her head about an inch to each side and spoke in a near-whisper. "No, Coach, I can hear you fine."

"Who are you?"

"Fortuna Jansel-Griffen, sir."

"What do you want, Fortuna Jansel-Griffen?"

"I want to do whatever the spirits require of me."

Lang frowned at that answer. "Dare I ask where you are from?"

"The spirits are silent on that issue."

"I wasn't asking the spirits. I was asking you, Fortuna Jansel-Griffen, where are you from?"

She swallowed hard. "I'm from the island of Aruba, a constituent country within the Kingdom of the Netherlands, which is a member of the European Union. So we're Dutch now, but we used to be Spanish, and before that we were Arawak."

"Is that all?" asked Lang.

Fortuna ground her right sneaker into the dirt. "I think we might have also been British for a while?"

"Take your laps!" Lang shouted.

Fortuna stumbled off to join the others, and only Tyler remained. Coach Lang stepped forward until he loomed over the Earth Team Captain. "I already know who you are, Tyler Sato. Of all the athletes on this team, only you can claim personal victories over M'Frozza the Mrendarian and Stonifer the Ossmendian."

Tyler felt his face flush at the two great accomplishments he couldn't take any credit for.

"Although I thought you'd be taller," Lang added.

"I get that a lot," said Tyler.

Coach Lang leaned in, close enough for Tyler to make out individual eyebrow hairs and the pores on the end of his nose. "What do you want, Captain Tyler?"

"I want—" Tyler took a breath that sank into his stomach like a metal weight. As far as he knew, nobody had ever challenged Auggie Lang, or mouthed off to him, or showed him any disrespect. Or at least, nobody who had survived. Tyler would have kept quiet as well, but sometimes words forced their way out through the defenses at the back of his throat. "I want you to stop tormenting my players."

At extreme close range, Lang's intense eyes had blood vessels that meandered like rivers, and brown flecks in the irises that exploded like starbursts. "Excuse me?" he asked.

"You must have scouting reports on every player. So what's with all the questions?"

Lang snarled angrily, or maybe his show of teeth was part of an unpracticed smile. "Two years ago, you played halfback on the Platte Bluff Coyotes, a town soccer team in your county's under-twelve league. You played an average of five minutes and thirty-seven seconds per game and kicked a total of three goals on the season, two of which were accidentally scored on your own net. Your coach had you pegged as a perennial bench-warmer, and yet here you are, a planetary captain in the Galaxy Games Tournament."

"Wait," said Tyler. "You spoke to my old coach?"

"The point is that scouting reports are incomplete. Yours, for example, fails to show your world-famous ability to dig deep into a vast reserve of hidden talent."

Very well hidden, Tyler thought. *So well hidden, it doesn't even exist!* He tried not to look away, but failed. Looking directly into Lang's face for any length of time was harder than looking directly at the sun.

"There's still one more answer I need from you, Captain Tyler."

Are you a fake? Are you a fraud? Are you a cheat? These were the questions Tyler expected, so he was relieved to get the same third question as everyone else. "Where are you from?"

"The United States?" Tyler guessed. "Nevada? Platte Bluff? Just tell me what you want me to say!"

Coach Lang shook his head. "Ten laps, Captain Tyler. Maybe you'll have the right answer for me next time."

1

In pine tree form, Ffargax reached deep into the underground network of roots and mycelium that carried the conversation of trees from across the human camp. The alpha vegetation on most worlds spent hundreds or thousands of cycles sharing their deepest thoughts, and Ffargax always felt privileged when they allowed him to listen in. It made him wish that more rooted species would register with the Galaxy Games Commission.

The spruce trees took bets on when it would rain again. A copse of white poplars on a nearby ridge rustled on and on about a pair of woodpeckers that had moved into the area. A jack pine went off on the poplars for being so cranky on overcast days, which caused a sugar maple to denounce all evergreens as self-righteous jerks.

Ffargax struggled to keep the sap running through his trunk. How could Earth trees be so boring? He'd met blades of tube-grass that could hold a better *conversation. Even worse, when Ffargax brought up the Galaxy Games Tournament, the Earth trees had no idea what he was talking about. They didn't know—or didn't care—that their world's champion had won a prime slot in the Pod Gizmo bracket. If Tyler Sato couldn't win fans among his own planet's trees, there really had to be something wrong with him.*

A fir tree overlooking the landing lot reported that the "insufferable human saplings" had returned, and that a new boss had them running around like dizzy chipmunks.

At first, Ffargax couldn't understand why the entire forest held the humans in such contempt. Then, gradually, he noticed their resentment was focused on the player cabins, crude shelters built from the tree-flesh planks of unwilling victims.

His pine needles quivered in horror!

A red oak announced when the Earth players were marching up the path of needlessly compressed soil, stomping on exposed roots as they went.

Ffargax felt the energy cannon weigh heavily on one of his branches. With luck, it would only take one shot to complete his mission.

8

"Where are you from? Where are you from? Where are you from?"

Coach Lang repeated the question over and over, and followed each out-of-breath answer with a demand for more laps, high-steps, skips, interval sprints, and other tortures.

Nobody earned chocolate cake.

Tyler dropped onto a growing pile of gasping players who also could not manage another step. Only a few kids were still jogging, led by Imara, a Kenyan distance runner who probably could have run all day without breaking a sweat.

Lang gave his head a disappointed shake. "You're dismissed. We'll resume after lunch."

The players groaned, but somehow they all found a way to stand, and to escape from the lot before Lang could change his mind. Tyler felt sore to his bones. He could barely lift his knees, and the player cabins felt like they were a million-mile hike away.

"Forget lunch," said Felix. "I'm sleeping until dinner."

"Wake me for breakfast tomorrow," said El Gatito.

"I don't want to sleep," said Baashi. "I'll just be having nightmares of Coach Lang shouting, 'Where are you from? Where are you from? Where are you from?'"

"*Where are you from?*" barked Maja, and Baashi took off into the nearest climbable tree.

"Not funny," said Felix, as Maja high-fived her giggling, snickering followers: Valya, Bader, Hari, Althea, and The Amazing Waldo. Even though Maja had dismissed the Mob from her service back in China, and a hundred times before that, they just kept coming back for more.

Maja and her Mob disappeared around the final bend in the path. Tyler waved the rest of the team onward as well, so that he could use the silence to coax Baashi back to the ground. "It's been a rough day for you," said Tyler, once the other boy's feet were firmly on the path.

Baashi shrugged. "There have been worse days, Captain Tyler, or so I've heard."

The two boys had almost reached the cabin-strewn clearing when they ran into a young pine tree in the middle of the path, where Tyler was pretty sure he'd never seen a pine tree before. "I must be even more tired than I thought," he stated through an eyes-closed yawn.

When he looked again, the pine tree had been replaced by a U.N. peacekeeper. The peacekeeper's left eye twitched, and for a moment, Tyler thought the man's cheeks had become translucent, revealing an oily liquid that swirled beneath his skin.

"I'm sorry," the peacekeeper said.

"For what?" Tyler stared dully at the shiny brass key in the peacekeeper's trembling hand. Was it something he was supposed to take? Tyler reached out his hand and took a few steps forward.

"I am so, so sorry." The peacekeeper slowly raised his key to eye-level and squeezed it tightly between his fingers—which was when Tyler suddenly tripped over a rock.

As Tyler tumbled onto the dirt path, something behind him popped like fireworks.

The other players came running from the direction of the cabins. "*¡Ay dios mío!*" El Gatito exclaimed. "A lightning strike!"

Tyler jumped to his feet and gaped at the smoldering tree trunks at the edge of the path. That bolt of lightning could have easily hit him or . . . Tyler looked all around. "Where's Baashi?"

"That coward?" Maja smirked. "He ran into the woods. He's probably cowering under a bush or something."

"Then you'd better go find him," said Tyler.

"Me?" Maja blinked. "But you're the captain."

"And you're the one who got him so worked up in the first place."

Tyler and Maja stood inches apart and glared into each other's eyes for a long moment. Finally, the Norwegian girl blinked and turned away. "Whatever you say, *Captain Tyler*." She spat his name out like a curse.

"And bring your Mob!" Tyler called, as Maja dropped the amber goggles over her face and stomped into the woods. Her five followers dutifully trailed after her.

Tyler grinned. Sometimes it was good to be the captain. "Maybe that peacekeeper can help us too."

"What peacekeeper?" asked Tomoko.

"The one standing right over—" Tyler turned, but the peacekeeper was gone. "Huh."

"Another alien abduction!" Weez exclaimed.

"You blame everything on aliens," said Tyler.

"That doesn't mean I'm wrong. It means I'm the only one with my eyes open, my friend." Weez stepped over to the smoldering tree trunks. "Like how I'm the only one who finds it strange when lightning strikes from a cloud-free sky."

Tyler had no answer for Weez, which bothered him more than the lightning itself.

9

Ffargax bubbled and fumed, too outraged to maintain a solid form. The sickening stench of charred wood still carried on the breeze. How could he have missed so badly? Hadn't he taken a shape the Earth boy was sure to trust? Hadn't he used a weapon no low-tech worldling would have ever seen? It would have taken blue-star reflexes for Captain Tyler to dodge that blast!

Could Dwogleys be responsible? Maybe the Order was right, and the Earth boy's invisible puppet-masters had sent him a warning. If Dwogleys did exist, they had sure used a clever strategy. Sap had been spilled, Ffargax was to blame, and the entire forest would now close ranks behind Captain Tyler. With one shot, Ffargax had lost the trees as his best and only allies on Earth.

Ffargax unpuddled into the form of a carnivorous mound-stalker, a native of Agalon III. He blended perfectly into the soil outside Captain Tyler's cabin, with the energy cannon tucked under his bulk for safekeeping.

While he waited, a squirrel wandered temptingly close. The mound-stalker's enzyme sack grumbled, but Ffargax had no time for chewing and swallowing a meal, not to mention the tedious digestion that would have to be done afterward. His mission came first, and a binge on fluff-tailed rodents would have to wait.

A few throbs passed.

The first squirrel was joined by a second, and the two of them scampered playfully around the clearing. Ffargax licked the froth from his mound-stalker maw, and refocused his attention on the cabin. It could not be much longer until his target emerged.

A dark-haired female peacekeeper walked up the path and knocked on the cabin door. Ffargax froze in place. Had the Earth boy called for military assistance? Or had the maple trees ratted him out? He held his oxygen intake as Captain Tyler opened the door and accepted a note—written on a bleached sheet of flattened tree pulp, of course. Ffargax simmered with renewed disgust at how these humans abused their trees.

"A video call? For me?" asked the Earth boy.

"That's right, Mr. Sato."

Captain Tyler scratched the back of his neck and yawned. "Thanks, Lieutenant Choi. I'll be there in a few minutes, okay?"

Peacekeeper Choi saluted and passed within a few feet of Ffargax on her way back down the trail. Luckily, she didn't seem to detect anything but dirt and leaves.

Once Choi had gone, Ffargax adjusted his mound-stalker body to expose the energy cannon's firing aperture. The safety clicked off, so that a simple squeeze would discharge the weapon. Surely, from his camouflaged position, Ffargax would be able to act before Captain Tyler or his Dwogleys could react.

The Earth boy went back inside. When he reemerged, Ffargax formed a magnifying eyespot and telephoto scope for targeting accuracy. As Captain Tyler approached along the path, Ffargax watched the Earth boy's head bob up and down.

Ffargax squeezed the discharge bulb until the energy cannon flared. The Earth boy's head disappeared. Mission accomplished.

"I hope you're happy, Spawn-Father," Ffargax spat. But when he readjusted his vision, he saw the Earth boy sprawled safely on the ground. A garbage bin on the far side of the cabin had broken into several charred and flaming chunks of metal. The Earth boy had dodged again!

Ffargax sprouted legs and charged forward in his human form to finish Tyler off at close range, but he was interrupted by a voice from further down the trail. "Hey!

What are you doing?"

Ffargax lowered his weapon and turned to address Peacekeeper Choi. She stood around the trail bend, visible to him but screened from the cabin by trees and undergrowth.

"Routine patrol duty, ma'am." Ffargax mentally smoothed the wrinkles from his uniform. The mesh of fibers, dye patterns, patches, and stitching looked genuine enough from a distance, but would it hold up to close inspection?

"You'd better come with me," said Choi.

Ffargax raised his energy cannon. He didn't want to hurt anyone except his target, but if the peacekeeper had seen him change shape, she could blow his cover and ruin his entire mission. Ffargax aimed, stepped forward, and— "Whoop!" Tripped over a rock. Before he could finish cursing the clumsiness of human legs, the enemy was at his side.

"Here, let me help you up," Choi said. "Are you hurt?"

"No, I'm just—" Ffargax stared down at his empty hands. "Oh no! I've dropped my energy cann—er, my good-luck charm."

"The key you were holding?" Choi frowned. "I hope it wasn't to anything important."

"Not at all," Ffargax said quickly. "It was just an

ordinary non-lethal piece of low-tech metal, but special to me because it belonged to my spawn-father."

The peacekeeper giggled.

"Did I say something funny?" asked Ffargax.

She rubbed the outside corner of her eye. "Sorry for laughing. You speak Korean very well for a Westerner, but some of your words come out a little strange."

"Ah, yes, Korean. That is the language of where you are from, and which we are speaking." Ffargax felt around the leafy ground for his energy cannon. Where could it have gone?

"I haven't seen you around before," said Choi. "Of course, that's no surprise, given all the turnover we've had in the ranks."

"Sure, right, turnover," he said, although the only turnover Ffargax cared about right then was turning over leaves to find his energy cannon. It really did belong to Spawn-Father, and there would be fire and pain if Ffargax lost it.

"We'll find your lucky charm later. Right now, we'd better run. The section chief's briefing starts in five minutes."

"There's a briefing?" Ffargax narrowed his eyes. "Why? Has the camp been infiltrated by a shape-shifter from another world? Um . . . that you know of?"

Choi giggled again. "You've been talking to that

spooky Weez kid, haven't you? Seriously though, the team has a new coach, there's another shift of chaperones, and some of us will be getting assignments off-planet during the tournament games. There are bound to be a whole lot of changes we'll all need to know about."

Ffargax considered this. His mission was taking longer than planned, and he was suddenly weaponless. It would benefit him to learn more about the camp's defenses. He nodded and followed Peacekeeper Choi down the trail.

Tyler ran a finger across his face, and winced at the fresh cut on his chin. Even on his clumsiest day, he'd never tripped over two completely different rocks before. Tyler pressed his shirt collar to the cut and waited for the bleeding to stop.

Through the trees, he could hear voices, and even some giggling, but his implant couldn't make out any words. His ears were ringing too loudly from something that had exploded nearby. He looked around and jumped at the sight of a fire burning itself out in the metal husk of a dumpster. Another lightning strike? Could the weather in Saskatchewan be that weird?

He looked for the rock that had tripped him, and tossed several likely suspects deeper into the woods. A few others were too deeply embedded in the ground for him to pry out with just his fingers. "Watch out, rocks. After I take this call, I'm coming back with a shovel!"

Tyler made his way, stepping more carefully, to the southwest corner of the camp. Next to the logistics center stood a large camouflage-fabric tent that served as the team's library, classroom, and computer center. Social media, news sites, and online games were filtered, to keep the team focused, but there were other games available, and off-duty players often used a video chat to call home.

"We found your Somali war hero," said Maja, without looking up from the first-person shooter on her screen. "He'd painted himself all over with mud, because it made great camouflage—or so he'd heard."

"Thanks," said Tyler.

Maja fired to make a kill. "Die, die, die!"

At another computer, The Amazing Waldo groaned as his dead character rezzed out and respawned. "Stop killing me, Maja. We're on the same team!"

Out of all the unused computers, Tyler took a seat at the one with the flickering screen of static. "Hello, Mom," he said into the microphone.

"Tyler!" came his mother's voice. "I haven't been able to get my picture working right. How did you know it was me?"

"Just a lucky guess. Have you tried switching the

camera on?"

"It has a switch?"

Tyler sighed. "Yes, Mom. It's in the back."

"I'm not seeing a switch there," said his mother. "Just a button. Am I looking for a switch or a button?"

"It might be a button," Tyler admitted.

The screen flared, and Tyler found himself looking into his own living room back home. He could see the bite marks along the edges of a wooden coffee table he'd defaced as a teething toddler, the ugly-patterned couch that looked better and better with every new spill or stain, and his mother's forehead and left eyebrow in the extreme foreground. Tyler felt so homesick, he was even glad to see his older sister with a mobile phone pressed against the side of her face.

"Hi, Amanda!" Tyler waved.

His sister kept talking on the phone.

"Amanda!" their mother snapped. "Say hi to your brother."

Amanda huffed. "Hold on a minute, Brandy." She put the phone aside. "Mom, I've got a more important conversation going on." Amanda brought the phone back to her face. "Sorry, Brandy. Now when you say Rick likes me, does he *like*-like me, or does he just *kinda*-like me?"

"Amanda really does miss you in her own way." His

mother peered closer into her screen. "Oh, honey bear! What happened to your face?"

Tyler glanced around and caught Maja mouthing the words, "Honey bear?" and The Great Waldo snickering back at her. The two of them whispered back and forth until Tyler had to turn away.

He put a hand to the cut he'd gotten from falling on the path. "It's nothing, Mom."

"It doesn't look like nothing. There's blood on your shirt collar! That's it, I'm calling your coach and telling him that you're coming home right now."

Tyler stared at the screen. "But Mom, I can't do that. I'm the planetary captain of the entire world!"

Tyler's mother sighed. "I know the Galaxy Games are important, but your safety is even more important."

"The Games are safe," Tyler insisted. "I have that advanced healing thing in my implant, and we'll be bringing a medical team with us everywhere we go. Besides, this cut doesn't have anything to do with the Games. There's been some weird weather, and I tripped over a rock. That could have happened anywhere, even back in Platte Bluff."

His mother raised an eyebrow. "You tripped over a rock?"

"Twice."

In the background, Amanda put down her phone. "I believe him, Mom. Nobody would make up a story about being that lame."

"Thanks, Amanda," Tyler grumbled.

His sister shrugged and went back to her phone call. "Nuh-uh! Those shoes look much better on me!"

"Has Dad left yet?" Tyler asked. "He's supposed to be here for Departure Day, but so far he hasn't shown up."

"Ah." His mother looked away. "That's actually why I called."

"What?" Tyler felt a lurch in his stomach. "Did anyone hurt him? Have they threatened you like they threatened Coach Graham's family?"

"No, honey bear. We're all safe."

"In a house that's safely surrounded by armed guards," Amanda mumbled from the middle of her own conversation. She looked left and right toward windows on either side of the living room.

"Dad was always supposed to go into space with me," Tyler said. "He can't have too much work to do. Not now."

"Honey bear, of course your father's been looking forward to this. There's nothing in the universe that could keep him from going with you . . . ordinarily."

"Ordinarily?"

From the distant background, Tyler could hear his father's voice ask, "Is that Tyler?"

"No, dear," Tyler's mother called. "Go back to bed."

"Don't lie to me, Naomi." Tyler's father stepped into the frame, wrapped in a blanket and with an ice pack on his head. Dr. Sato coughed for several seconds before asking, "How are you doing, kiddo?"

"Better than you, apparently," said Tyler.

"What, you mean this?" His father gestured to the ice pack. "I'm fighting off a slight fever. I'll be one hundred percent healthy again by the time that shark-shaped bus swoops down to pick me up."

"Hiroshi Sato," Tyler's mother scolded.

"Well, maybe more like eighty percent healthy, but that's still a solid B-minus of health." Tyler's father put a tissue to his nose and blew like a trumpet. "Okay. Would you believe sixty percent?"

"How are you going to fly into space?" Tyler's mother asked. "I'm pretty sure you need to pass a physical, and you could barely drag yourself into the bathroom this morning."

"I'll find a way." Tyler's father erupted into another coughing fit and stumbled out of the room.

"So you'll be coming with us to space instead?" Tyler asked his mother, hopefully.

She shook her head. "I can't take a week off of work

on such short notice. Besides, your father will never recover unless I'm here to nurse him back to health."

"But one of you has to come," Tyler insisted.

Amanda put down her phone. "Fine," she said.

"What's fine?" asked their mother.

"I'll do it," said Amanda. "I'll help chaperone Tyler and his stupid friends on their stupid trip into stupid outer space."

"It's not nice to call things stupid," said their mother.

Amanda shrugged. "Whatever."

"Wait." Tyler struggled to process his sister's words without spraining his brain. "You want to come with us? But you can't! We need an adult."

"I just turned eighteen, so I'm totally an adult now. I can vote and everything! Plus I know CPR, and I have years of experience as a babysitter."

"I don't need a babysitter!" Tyler shouted.

"This might not be such a good idea," said their mother.

"Come on, Mom," said Amanda. "There'll be lots of other adults around, and it's totally unfair to make me stay behind when Tyler and Cousin Daiki both get to go."

"Please, please, please don't let Amanda come with me," Tyler begged. "She'll ruin everything! Ask Eric's mother. Or Brayden's father. Or my old soccer coach. There has to be one responsible adult in the entire city of Platte Bluff!"

"Your sister does have a point," their mother said. "If we're letting you go into space, we have to let her go as well. And Amanda can be very mature when she has to be."

Amanda stuck her tongue out at Tyler but snapped into in an angel-innocent pose by the time their mother turned around.

"I'll discuss it with your father," said Mom.

"And I'll pack a suitcase!" Amanda exclaimed.

Tyler couldn't focus on anything else his mom said. Not with the whole room spinning around at the thought of Amanda going with him into space. "Nothing could be more embarrassing," he said, after closing the chat window.

Then Maja waved to him from the exit. "See you at lunch, *Captain Honey Bear*!"

Twelve seconds. That was how long Tyler spent in his seat, in front of a heaping serving of cheese lasagna, before Maja shouted to him from across the crowded Café Terra dining hall. "Hey, Captain Honey Bear!"

"Shut up, Maja!" Tyler shouted back.

Maja laughed, and Valya, Bader, Hari, Althea, and The Great Waldo laughed along with her.

"What's that all about?" asked Felix, and the Challengers at Tyler's table leaned inward like football players in a huddle.

"Moms," said Tyler. "Do they have to practice to become so embarrassing, or does it come naturally?"

"I wouldn't know," said Felix, a little stiffly. "I live with my dad."

"I live with *Obaa-chan*," said Tomoko.

"El Gatito lives with a sense of mystery and adventure!" the masked wrestler proclaimed.

Ling-Wa jabbed at her rice bowl with chopstick pincers. "There is a woman who calls herself my mother. I'd be happy to never see her again."

"Okay then," said Tyler. "I guess I'm kind of lucky when it comes to moms, but also still embarrassed."

"Mmph." Weez swallowed a bite of his Bauru sandwich, although a chunk of crust still clung to the side of his face, dangling a piece of roast beef from a string of mozzarella. "Dude, I've seen your mom on TV. That time when she chased a dozen reporters off your front lawn? In her bathrobe? While waving a toilet brush around? She terrifies me."

The other Challengers nodded.

A chunk of jellied whitefish crashed onto the table from above, scattering the lunch plates and silverware. Tomato sauce splashed onto Tyler's shirt and face.

Tyler jumped to his feet. "Maja!"

Across the room, Maja looked up from her plate with a mock-innocent expression. "Me?"

"I know it was you, Maja. Nobody else would touch your lutefisk with a ten-foot pole!"

Maja shrugged. "Sorry, Captain Tyler. It must have slipped out of my hand."

Tyler and Maja glared at each other across a dining hall of players with tense fingers on their plates, ready for the food fight of the century.

At that moment, Coach Lang strode through the room with a tray of sloppy joe balanced on one hand. He addressed the room with a scowl. "I realize I'm still new here, but I will not have two factions of my team at each other's throats in the middle of the dining hall. Understood?"

"Yes, sir," said Tyler.

"Yes, sir," said Maja.

"Yes, sir," said each individual member of the Challengers and the Mob.

"Good. If you're going to be at each other's throats, let's make sure it happens at a proper venue. This table and that table—" Lang pointed from Tyler and his Challengers to Maja and her Mob. "—will meet on the field of battle at Chichén Itzá, first thing after lunch."

Lang continued onward to a table of administrative staffers, and dug into his meal.

Tyler fell back into his seat. He didn't want to fight with Maja at all, but at least this way he'd get to finish his food. "What's a Chichén Itzá?"

"It's in the Yucatan," El Gatito stated between bites of his black bean burrito.

"And what does that mean?" asked Tomoko.

The Mexican *luchador* grinned. "My family has deep connections to the Yucatan. We were Mayan, once. So home field advantage for me!"

12

CHICHÉN ITZÁ, YUCATÁN, MEXICO:

A holographic Galaxy Games scoreboard covered the open skies above an ancient Mesoamerican ball court. The nine-box grid of swiftly-shifting X's and O's resembled a game of Tic-Tac-Toe gone wild, because "Tic-Tac-Toe Gone Wild" was a good description of the official sport, contest, wager, and challenge of the million-plus worlds of Galactic Civilization.

Under the scoreboard, between a pair of twenty-eight-foot walls, the grassy court stretched longer and wider than a football field. Tyler stood with his team of Challengers at one end, while Maja and her Mob hurled insults and catcalls from across the center line.

"What's your problem?" Tyler asked.

"You are!" Maja shouted.

"That makes no sense, Maja!"

"The Great and Mighty Tyler Sato," Maja jeered, as

if that explained anything. Tyler couldn't tell whether she'd even meant it as an insult. Maja's Mob was split on the matter as well; Hari and Bader cheered while Althea and Valya booed, and The Amazing Waldo turned an awkward double-somersault.

"I'm not great *or* mighty," Tyler grumbled to himself.

"Well, *duh*," said Weez.

Tyler glared. "You don't have to agree with me."

"Just being truthful, dude." The Brazilian soccer star popped a stick of gum into his mouth. "You're not the fastest runner on the team, or the highest jumper, or the farthest thrower, or the strongest fighter, or the most coordinated. I mean honestly, you can barely walk down a dirt path without tripping over a rock."

Tyler rubbed his chin. The cut no longer hurt, thanks to the healing power of his implant, but he still winced at the memory of his pain. "I thought you were supposed to be on my side."

"Always," said Weez. "Because there's one thing you do better than anyone else in the world."

Tyler waited. And waited. And waited.

Weez chewed his gum, blew a bubble, and chewed some more.

Finally, Tyler cleared his throat.

"Hmm?" asked Weez.

"What is the one thing I do better at than anyone else in the world?" Tyler demanded.

"Oh, I thought that was obvious. You, Tyler Sato, are able to stand in the center of the brightest media spotlight on Planet Earth—month after month after month—and it hasn't turned you into a total jerk." Weez popped another bubble. "Or at least, not yet."

Tyler's shoulders slumped. "Is that all?"

"See?" Weez asked. "You're so modest! That's why Maja hates you, and why the rest of us think you're so great. It's also cool that aliens contact you first when they come to Earth. Because if those aliens are ever the ones who took my brother, I'll be with you to hear about it." Weez rubbed his hands together and cackled.

Tyler backed away slowly. Weez might not have been quite as crazy as he looked, but there was still no reason to encourage him.

Tomoko ran up, nearly knocking Tyler over. "*Sempai*, we've got a problem!"

Before Tyler could ask what she meant, Ling-Wa stumbled past with an enormous golden headdress-helmet sticking two feet up from the top of her head. Tufts of feathers fluttered, tiny bells jangled, and Ling-Wa nearly crashed into a wall before Tyler got to her. The Mayan ballplayers carved onto that wall from ancient times wore similar headgear, but they had managed to keep theirs from falling over their eyes.

Together with Felix, Tyler pulled the helmet upward until Ling-Wa could see again. "Problem solved," Tyler announced.

Tomoko shook her head. "That's not our only problem." She pointed to the corner of the field, where other headdress-helmets were arranged into a huge pile, along with feather-coated chest protectors, hip-pads, yoke-shaped belts, and brightly-colored elbow- and knee-pads. At the top of that pile, El Gatito stood like a mountain climber, and crowed like a rooster.

El Gatito still wore his blue cat-eared mask, as always, but he had replaced his wrestling leotard and cape with a full set of Mayan regalia.

"The spirit of El Gatito's Mayan ancestors will guide us to victory," he announced.

"Why is El Gatito wearing a loincloth?" Tyler wondered. "And how did he put it on without a changing room?"

Tomoko shuddered. "It's best not to ask."

El Gatito continued to pose and preen while both teams strapped the Mayan-themed protective gear over their practice uniforms. Nobody else opted for a loincloth, although several were available.

Coach Lang stepped out to half-court, turning a small soccer ball over and over in his hands. The two teams assembled on either side. Maja's Mob glared at Tyler, while Tyler's Challengers glared back at Maja.

Above the stadium, the X's and O's vanished, leaving an empty Tic-Tac-Toe grid.

"The rules of the game are simple," Lang stated. There were no other instructions. Lang dropped the ball onto the grass and walked to the spectator gallery, where an air-horn announced the start of the game.

Tyler looked around at the rest of his players: Felix and Tomoko shrugged back at him; Weez was peeking at a nearby step-pyramid while muttering about Ancient Astronauts; El Gatito was running along the side wall, high-fiving the Mayan ballplayers carved onto the panels; and Ling-Wa was pulling her helmet back up from where it had fallen over her eyes again.

Tyler's only consolation was that Maja and her Mob seemed equally confused.

Tyler stepped forward and kicked the ball as hard as he could. His foot erupted in pain, as if he had kicked a football-sized rock. The ball that had seemed so light in Coach Lang's hands was solid rubber, and the thin cushioning of Tyler's Falcon Zero-Weights offered no protection for his toes.

The ball slow-rolled eighteen inches into Maja's territory.

"Good one, *Captain Honey Bear*." Maja sneered at

Tyler. Then she looked up at all the cheering from the spectator gallery. The other Galaxy Games players were going nuts over something.

"Tyler-san! We're winning!" Tomoko exclaimed.

Tyler looked up at two fresh blue X's in the Northern Edge and Southeast Corner boxes of the scoreboard. Faint blue lines showed the Challengers' advantage in two verticals, two horizontals, and one diagonal. "Whatever you did, just keep doing it," said Felix, as if Tyler had that many unbroken toes.

"Oh no you don't!" Maja booted the ball from the other side, and her own shrieks of pain could have sent axe-wielding warriors running for cover. The ball rolled back across the center line. The two blue X's became red O's, one after the other, and the faint blue lines turned faintly pink.

Maja hopped up and down next to Tyler, who was also hopping on his uninjured foot. They both grimaced in pain as bells jangled on their Mayan headdress-helmets. "See, Honey Bear? You'll never beat a Viking at a toe-breaking contest!"

"But that can't be what this is," said Tyler.

Felix and Bader approached the ball cautiously from either side. Bader reached down to pick it up. "Mine!" he exclaimed. But as soon as Bader's fingers touched the ball, he seized up and fell over like a frozen statue.

"You can never touch the ball with your hands," El Gatito called. "That part should have been obvious."

Felix placed a foot on top of the ball, and the Northern Edge box flipped from a red O back to a blue X. "Last-touch gets that one square, and the other must depend on what side of the field the ball is on." With the sole of his sneaker, he rolled the ball past Bader's frozen body. At the center line, the second red O instantly turned back into a blue X as well.

Tyler nodded, glad that El Gatito knew the rules and that Felix could figure out the scoring. In some sessions of the Galaxy Games, the rules were known in advance. In some sessions, the rules were invented and changed as the game went on. But in some sessions, the rules were known only to the scorekeeper and had to be discovered during play.

The Challengers and the Mob players converged on the ball, using their feet and legs to move it around. "Althea!" Maja snapped. "You don't have toes to worry about. Go kick that ball extra hard."

Althea hung back, scraping at the turf with the carbon-fibre blades on the stubs of her amputated legs. "But I didn't bring my kicking feet. These are running blades, and I got them brand new for the tournament."

Maja rolled her eyes. "So you weren't thinking

about me and my needs when you were selecting your artificial feet? That's really selfish, Althea."

Althea clicked the curved black blades together. "Sorry."

The ball moved back and forth, and the same two squares traded back and forth on the scoreboard. Tyler's Challengers had an advantage until Bader unfroze from his penalty and rejoined the game, seemingly unharmed.

Then out of nowhere, Hari and the Amazing Waldo charged at the ball with a pair of curved black sticks.

"Were those in the equipment pile?" Tyler asked.

"Not that El Gatito noticed." The cat-eared wrestler scratched the forehead of his mask.

"So where did they get them?"

"I have no idea, *El Capitán*. El Gatito is stumped."

"No, *I'm* stumped," said Althea. She stood on her knees and the stumps of her lower legs. Without her prostheses, she looked like she were stuck in a hole.

"Oh! El Gatito is so sorry!"

"Not as sorry as those boys are going to be if they damage my feet. My parents are still making payments on that pair!"

Hari hooked one of Althea's foot-blades under the ball and scooped it into the air. A red O appeared in the previously-empty Eastern Edge box of the scoreboard to mark a ball sent airborne.

The ball slammed into Ling-Wa's chest-protector, knocking her to the turf. A blue X appeared in the previously-empty Northwest Corner box to mark a ball played off the chest.

After that, the ball went airborne more frequently and more intentionally, travelled farther, bounced off different pieces of protective gear, and lit up additional boxes on the scoreboard. Soon, only the Western Edge and Center boxes remained stubbornly empty, and the three-in-a-row winning condition eluded both sides.

El Gatito slid up to Tyler's side as he, Weez, and Tomoko battled Hari, Waldo, and Valya for control of the ball. "El Gatito has figured out how to win the Center," the masked wrestler whispered.

"How?" asked Tomoko.

El Gatito nodded upward at a stone ring mounted near the top of the twenty-eight-foot wall.

Tyler's brain boggled at the thought of getting such a heavy object through such a high target. "Any idea how we'd kick the ball all the way up there?"

"Oh, I know," said Weez.

Tyler, Tomoko, and El Gatito waited. And waited.

Weez chewed his gum thoughtfully. He blew a bubble that popped against his face. Then he peeled the filmy gum from his nose, popped it back into his mouth, and chewed it some more.

"How?" Tyler demanded.

"Oh, right, that. Well, obviously, we'll need to locate the Ancient Astronauts who built this ball court and enlist their help."

Tomoko rolled her eyes. "Obviously."

"The Mayans built this place," El Gatito stated.

"Without having first invented the wheel?" asked Weez. "They must have had extraterrestrial help."

"Don't insult El Gatito's ancestor spirits. They could have used wheels if they'd wanted to. They just didn't want to make things too easy for themselves."

"Whatever. I'm going to check for Ancient Astronauts at the top of that step-pyramid."

"Wait!" Tyler called, but Weez was already trotting off the field. "Great, now we're down a player."

El Gatito dropped to one knee. "Forgive my ignorant teammate, mighty ancestor spirits. Weez has the heart of a warrior, but the brain of a squirrel."

Valya maneuvered past Tomoko and kicked the ball across the center line for Maja's Mob, turning the Northern Edge box from an X to an O.

"El Gatito to the rescue!" The masked *luchador* flipped the ball into the air, bounced it off the center of his hip-pad, and watched the ball catch fire.

Literally.

In a halo of crackling blue flames, the ball shot off El Gatito's hip, directly at Felix. The soccer goalie tried to deflect the ball with his hands, but only managed to tip it upward slightly. The flaming ball bounced hard off the wall, ricocheted back, and dented the ground about three feet from where El Gatito had fielded it.

A blue X lit up in the previously-empty Western Edge box to mark the unlocked achievement.

Every player on the field stood frozen in amazement, except for Felix, who stood frozen because he'd touched the ball with his hands.

"That was impossible!" Maja exclaimed.

The blue flames sparked out, and the ball regained its dull-gray rubbery appearance as if nothing had ever happened.

"How did he do that?" Tomoko asked.

"Do what?" Ling-Wa pushed the headdress-helmet off her eyes again. "Did I miss something? Hey, where's Weez? And why is everyone just standing around?"

El Gatito touched the Mayan figures painted on his hip-pad. "El Gatito thanks you, great ancestor spirits. Your help is timely, and your fire is fierce!"

"No fair!" shouted Hari. "I want ancestor spirits in *my* protective gear!"

Tyler looked down at his own hip-pad, which looked identical to El Gatito's in every way. It was molded from the same hard plastic, with foam on the inside and colorfully-painted Mayan-themed designs on the outside. And yet, the ball had already bounced off Tyler's hip several times during the game without turning into a flaming blue ball of death, and he had the bruises to prove it.

"What did El Gatito do differently from the rest of us?" Tyler asked.

"It must be the loincloth!" Maja exclaimed. "Bader, Hari, Annoying Waldo, get back to the equipment pile and put on some loincloths."

"Um, it's the *Amazing* Waldo," Waldo corrected her. "And there's no changing room."

"Just go," Maja snapped, "or my wrath will descend upon you like a thousand Viking longboats!"

The three boys hustled downfield at top speed, and Althea took the opportunity to reclaim her feet.

Tyler took a closer look at the hip-pad designs. There were swirls and animals, ballplayers in elaborate costume, and at the center of it all, a bright blue star.

"Aren't you going to put on a loincloth?" Ling-Wa asked him.

Tyler grinned. "I don't need to. I've already figured out how to win the game."

13

CAMP GALAXY, SASKATCHEWAN, CANADA:

By the end of the short security briefing, Ffargax had learned the layout of the camp, the schedule of the team, and the operations of the security force. Best of all, he learned that none of the peacekeepers were expecting a shape-shifting alien assassin to infiltrate their ranks. Somehow, they hadn't even considered the possibility!

Ffargax had some time to kill before his time to kill, so he explored the forest from above, soaring high in the form of a turkey vulture. He'd had to reinforce and lengthen the wings to get his entire bulk into the air, but the oblivious humans he'd met so far would never notice the difference.

The Earth team was away for the afternoon—or so Ffargax thought, until he spotted Captain Tyler sitting on a tree stump in the middle of a small clearing. Ffargax narrowed his avian eyes. The Earth boy was using a *noble tree's remains as his own personal outdoor throne! Such arrogance could hardly go unpunished.*

Captain Tyler sat alone, without any teammates or security guards. Ffargax found that suspicious, but circling from above revealed no obvious traps. Without Spawn-Father's energy cannon, Ffargax would have to fall back on a shape-shifter's selection of natural weapons: claws, probe spikes, teeth, needle jets, smother-skins, and such. There were plenty of options a human target wouldn't be able to dodge or avoid, if Ffargax could get close enough to use them.

He landed silently at the edge of the clearing.

The human boy held a controller with knobs and buttons that moved a red and blue human-shaped toy along the ground. Ffargax watched for a while as the doll hopped around, kicked turtle shells out of its way, and travelled across an elaborate structure of bricks and boxes. It seemed like a strange hobby for a Galaxy Games captain, but Ffargax was hardly one to judge. After all, his own hobbies included socializing with trees and attempted murder.

Ffargax crept forward in the form of a Wilnarian turf-mimic. It felt weird to mimic a thing that mimicked another thing, but the clever turf-mimic was the sneakiest predator Ffargax could think of, a creature that could move through a herd of herbivores and gnaw their faces off as they bent down to graze.

After a few pulses, Ffargax got close enough to see that this human boy wasn't Tyler Sato at all, but a close substitute. A very close substitute. If Ffargax hadn't so naturally attuned to slight differences of shape and tone, he might have even been fooled.

Could this boy have been placed in the forest as a decoy?

Ffargax flared his senses up and down the spectrum but could detect no surveillance equipment. This boy was probably just a pod-brother, half-clone, or other close relative to Tyler Sato.

The jumping doll bopped its head repeatedly against the underside of a box that dangled from the tree branches overhead. A plastic mushroom dropped to the forest floor. Another box produced a golden disk. The human boy was so distracted by his efforts that he failed to notice a patch of grass shift into the shape of a peacekeeper.

Ffargax cleared his throat to announce his presence.

"Nani?" The boy dropped the controller and looked up. "Oh! I didn't see you there."

Ffargax smiled his most reassuring smile, still ready to run if his approach triggered a trap.

"Excuse me." The human boy retrieved his red-and-blue doll and returned with it to the stump.

Ffargax nodded at the controller. "You're pretty good with that thing."

"Thank you." The boy opened a compartment in the doll's head and pulled out a spherical camera drone. "With my drone inside a Mario-shaped piñata, I can move it around by remote control. The boxes took a long time to set up, but it's just like Super Mario Brothers in real life! And if M'Frozza brings us a second drone, I can build a Luigi."

Ffargax froze. How had he overlooked a camera drone hidden inside the doll? Its quantum signal could have been broadcasting all across the galaxy. The peacekeepers were probably watching the live feed, preparing a strike force, and—

"Don't worry. It's not filming right now," said the boy. "But when I go into space with Cousin Tyler-kun and the others, I'll be able to send all the highlights back to Earth!"

Cousin Tyler-kun. *Ffargax's language implant registered the relationship and the familiar form of address. "Ah, then Tyler is the child of one or more siblings of your parent or parents. And what is your name?"*

"Daiki." The boy pointed a finger to his own nose. Then he blinked and narrowed his eyes. "But you would know that already, if you were a real peacekeeper."

Daiki's eyes widened. "You must be an imposter!"

The human boy grabbed his doll, tucked the drone under his armpit, and ran.

Ffargax felt a wave of panic ripple through his plasmic fluids. If this boy gave him away, his entire mission would fail. The Messenger would survive! The Galaxy Games would be ruined by Dwogleys! And also, Spawn-Father would be very angry.

Ffargax leapt forward and caught up with Daiki before he reached the forest path. Pulling the human boy off his feet was easy, but Ffargax had trouble pinning Daiki's shoulders to the ground. Although Ffargax had the form and size of an adult human, his natural mass was only a little more than Daiki's.

"Help! Help! Seclusionists!" Daiki shouted.

"Quiet!" Ffargax became a South Fervian strangle-vine and slapped a broad leaf over Daiki's mouth. Meanwhile, his tendrils wrapped around the boy's chest and squeezed until all protests stopped.

The Mario piñata fell to the ground and shattered, and Daiki's body slumped over on top of it.

Ffargax pulled away. "Oh, no! No, no, no! Look what you made me do!" He fanned Daiki's face with one of his leaves, but the boy was no longer breathing.

14

CHICHÉN ITZÁ, YUCATÁN, MEXICO:

The Mob boys moved with less confidence in their loincloths, which put the Challengers on a better footing: Felix unfroze from his penalty; Tyler took on Maja; Tomoko faced off against Valya; El Gatito continued to attack the ball with all the fury of his ancestor spirits; and Ling-Wa struggled to keep the headdress-helmet from falling down over her eyes.

And somewhere else on the plaza, Weez was still on his mission to find the Ancient Astronauts.

For several minutes, neither team managed to score three consecutive boxes along an edge of the giant scoreboard in the sky.

Tyler watched carefully any time a player bounced the ball off the top, bottom, or sides of a hip-pad. The ball sometimes came close to hitting the blue star, but it hadn't, and it also hadn't turned into a flaming rocketball again, either.

While Felix powered the ball past Bader and Hari, Tomoko hung back. "We need the center square to the win," she told Tyler. "What's your plan?"

"In situations like this, don't you always like to ask what Hunter-Elf Zeita would do?"

Tomoko narrowed her eyes. "Don't mess with me, *Sempai.*"

"Really," said Tyler. "If Zeita were here, she'd grab her longbow, select a magical arrow, and take a wild shot."

"So we're going to—?"

"Take a wild shot. When I give you the signal, kick the ball at me, about waist-high."

"*Hai, Sempai!*" Tomoko saluted as crisply as any naval midshipman. Then she frowned. "Did you mean *your* waist-high or *my* waist-high?"

Tyler scowled up at her. "*My* waist-high."

"Got it. That's what I'd thought, but it never hurts to check."

Tyler threw himself back into the game. He took a pass from El Gatito, and found himself on the other side of the ball from Maja.

"I thought your Challengers would have put this game away by now," she sneered. "What's wrong, Captain? Have you gone soft, or am I just that much better than Stonifer the Ossmendian?"

"I know Stonifer. I've played against Stonifer. I've beaten Stonifer. And guess what, Maja? You're no Stonifer!" Tyler rolled the ball left and right with a series of top-kicks. His right foot was still tender from the first hard kick of the game, but the healing factor in his implant must have been hard at work because his toes felt more bruised and less broken. "I sent Weez away to give your team a fighting chance, and we're still just toying with you."

"Oh yeah? Well . . . *Viking blood!*" Maja tried to stomp the ball, but lost her balance and fell over.

"Try not to get your Viking blood all over my clean uniform."

Maja looked like she was about to explode. She charged forward and got a foot between Tyler and the ball, sweeping it back toward her side of the field. "Tell you what, Captain Honey Bear. Let's make this interesting."

Tyler looked around. "We're playing in a thousand-year-old Mayan stadium with a ball that sometimes catches on fire and a scoreboard that blocks out the sun. How much more interesting can it get?"

"I'm talking about a wager. If my team wins, I get a seat at the Captain's Table."

"The what?" asked Tyler.

"The Captain's Table. You know, your table at Café Terra. If my team wins, I get to sit with you and the Challengers and lord it over everyone else in the Camp Galaxy dining hall!"

"But you can already do that," said Tyler.

"What?" Maja stumbled, and Tyler took back control of the ball.

"There are no assigned tables at Café Terra. If you wanted to sit with us, any day in the past two years, you could have just pulled up a seat. Vikings aren't supposed to be so shy."

Maja clenched her fists. "I'm not shy!"

"Of course not. Now here's what I want from this wager. When my team wins—and we will win—I want you to stop acting like such a jerk. No more insults, no more snide comments, and no more lunchtime lutefisk missiles."

"That's a deal, *Captain Honey Bear*." She smiled at his raised eyebrows. "I can still say that for now. You haven't beaten us yet."

Tyler looked up at the stone ring on the wall. He'd been working the ball toward it during his conversation with Maja, until he'd reached the perfect position on the field. "Now!" he shouted to Tomoko, as he pushed the ball toward her with his heel.

Tomoko got the ball into the air and launched it

forward with a karate kick that would have made Mr. Miyagi happier than all the waxed cars and painted fences in the world. "Oops!" Tomoko proclaimed.

Tyler pivoted his body to aim the blue star on his hip-pad toward the stone ring. *Oops?* That was a strange thing for Tomoko to say. And wasn't the ball coming at him way too high? Even if he jumped up, the ball was still going to hit him right in the—

Slam!

The heavy ball whacked Tyler in the head, and all he could see were stars and darkness.

15

PLATTE BLUFF, NEVADA, USA:

"Your shot, dude."

Tyler got his hands up just in time to catch the ball before it hit him in the face. He'd been expecting something heavier, but this was just an ordinary basketball. Tyler rubbed the pebbled rubber surface with his fingertips just to make sure.

"C'mon, Tyler. It's the last play of the day before my mom calls me in for dinner. You're welcome to stay if you want—there's no meat in the pasta sauce tonight, I promise. Just take the shot, okay?"

Tyler followed the voice across the blacktop to the fence where a familiar boy tapped his foot impatiently. "Eric? Eric Parker?"

"Stop stalling," said Eric. "You know you're going to choke on this shot, I know you're going to choke on this shot, but you still have to put that brick in the air."

Tyler gave the ball an experimental dribble. If this was a dream, it sure felt real, like he really was back in Platte Bluff at his best friend's driveway basketball hoop. "Eric, I've got a question for you and it's going to sound a little weird."

"Dude, all your questions sound weird. What's up?"

Tyler swallowed a lump in his throat. "Am I someone famous?" he asked. "Like, am I the most famous athlete in the history of the world?"

Eric snorted. Then chuckled. Then fell over himself laughing. "Dude! Where do you get this stuff?"

"I was just asking." Tyler gave the ball another bounce. "So there was no doomsday asteroid that turned out to be an alien spaceship? No Easter Island statues on the Moon? No Seclusionist terror attack in Athens?"

Eric stopped laughing. "What's a Seclusionist? Seriously, did you get hit in the head or something?"

"I'm not sure." Tyler rubbed the spot on his head where he thought he'd just been hit by a heavy ball.

In an ancient Mayan ball court.

While training for a sports tournament in outer space.

Which all sounded pretty crazy when he thought about it. "Hey, Eric? Have you ever heard of the Galaxy Games?"

"Is that a new video game?" asked Eric.

"No, it's nothing. Don't worry about it." Tyler took a few short breaths. "So, what shot am I taking?"

"Trick shot for the win," said Eric, "as if you'd forgotten. Bounce it off your head, off your hip, and into the basket."

Tyler laughed. "Easy!" On Eric's driveway, and pretty much nowhere else, Tyler was master of the court. He won every game of one-on-one, every game of twenty-one, every game of horse, and no trick shot was beyond his command. Two bounces. Look at the hoop. Two more bounces, and—

"Wait," said Eric.

Tyler pulled to a hard stop. "Really? After rushing my shot, now you're going to hold me back? You must really want to jinx me."

"It's my turn to ask a question, while I have you here."

Tyler frowned and gave Eric a closer look. His best friend's eyes had gone strangely dull, with flecks of light reflected from deep inside. He wouldn't say anything out loud, but it kind of creeped him out. "Okay."

"What if you could have a do-over? What if you could choose to be here, in your old life, instead of . . . elsewhere?"

"You mean instead of being back in my weird Galaxy Games dream?" Tyler asked.

"Exactly."

Tyler thought for a moment. "I love space, all the stars and planets, the astronomy my father studies, and the really weird stuff like black holes and dark matter. Imagine all the different types of alien life that could be scattered across a huge galaxy like ours. It would be amazing to explore it all first hand, but of course that's stupid. I'm just an ordinary kid."

"It's not stupid," said Eric. "And there's no such thing as an ordinary kid."

"Okay, now who's acting weird?" asked Tyler.

"Just take your shot."

Tyler nodded. Two bounces, a look at the hoop, two more bounces, and he tossed the ball up about a foot over his head. One bounce off his temple, one bounce off his thrusting hip, and through the hoop touching nothing but net.

"In your face!" Tyler shouted. "I'm the king of the driveway! I'm the pride of Platte Bluff! I am the Great and Mighty Tyler Sato, Planetary Captain, Lunar Explorer, Slayer of Stone-Boys, and Tamer of Squid-Girls!"

"Yes you are," said Eric Parker, as he and the rest of Platte Bluff melted away.

16

CHICHÉN ITZÁ, YUCATÁN, MEXICO:

Tyler opened his eyes to the concerned face of Dr. Luchenkov. "Do you know who you are?" the team doctor asked.

"Am I someone famous?"

"Most people would say so."

"Then I must be Tyler Sato," said Tyler.

"Good." Dr. Luchenkov nodded. "Do you know what day it is?"

Tyler pushed himself up on his arms. Beyond the doctor, he could see his worried teammates and the impassive face of Coach Lang. They were all still in the Great Ball Court, so he couldn't have been knocked out for very long. "I haven't missed Departure Day, have I? That's still tomorrow, right?"

"Yes. Again, this is good. It would be unfortunate to risk serious concussion at such an important time, *da*?" The doctor turned to glare at Coach Lang before looking back. "One more thing, Tyler. Do you know what you have just done?"

Tyler looked up at the sky. A blue X had appeared in the center square of the scoreboard, along with a flashing white line showing where the Challengers had scored three in a row to win the match. Tyler grinned. "I launched that ball off my head, off my hip, and through the hoop like a flaming blue star."

Dr. Luchenkov sighed. "When I worked on International Space Station, among astronauts and cosmonauts I could never say who had the hardest heads. Then I met you kids, and now I know. Take it easy until your healing factor kicks in, and I will do tests, *da*? If you pass, I give medical clearance for you to depart with your team."

"Thanks, Doc."

Dr. Luchenkov picked up his black bag and strode off the field. Tyler was immediately swarmed by other players. "That was awesome!" shouted Hari. "If we had to lose to Tyler's Challengers, I'm glad it was in such a cool way." Valya, Bader, Althea, and the Amazing Waldo hooted and cheered in agreement.

"Thanks," said Tyler. "It was just a wild shot I cooked up with Tomoko. Right, Tomoko?"

"Um, yeah." Tomoko laughed nervously and

scratched her arm. "And it happened exactly like we'd planned it. Kind of. Sorry about your head, though."

"Don't worry about it."

Weez jogged up to the group. "Captain Tyler! I couldn't find the Ancient Astronauts anywhere, but hey! Did we win?"

"Oh, man! You missed the most amazing shot! Bam, wham, kick!" El Gatito jumped, flipped, and made everyone else wish he were wearing more than just a loincloth. "The spirit of El Gatito's ancestors infused Tyler with the most unearthly powers!"

"Unearthly powers?" asked Weez. "Wait. Are you saying your ancestors *are* the Ancient Astronauts?"

"El Gatito isn't saying anything. El Gatito needs to maintain his sense of mystique."

Tyler looked down at the Mayan designs on his padding. He didn't believe in Ancient Astronauts or ancestral spirits, but *something* in that dream had looked out at him through Eric Parker's eyes.

"Captain Tyler!" Coach Lang snapped.

Tyler jumped to his feet. "The United States! Nevada! Japan! Timbuktu! Just tell me what you want to hear!"

Lang frowned. "It's sad to not know where you're from, but my question for you this time is, were you expecting a message?"

Tyler shook his head, and winced at the dull pain that rattled his brain.

"This . . . object arrived while you were playing." Lang held out a glowing blue cube, about the size of an apple. In the air next to the box, two piercing red stars stared out from a holographic black cloud. It was the image of a Galaxy Games Commissioner, like the ones that oversaw Tyler's official challenges against M'Frozza and Stonifer.

Next to the box on the other side, a hologram of Tyler's head spun like a sterling silver pendant on the Home Shopping Channel. Tiny specks of light, like dust caught in a sunbeam, flowed from the Commissioner's image into the box, and from the box to the spinning Tyler-head.

"That does look like a message for me," Tyler agreed. He accepted the cube, which turned from blue to green as it touched the skin of his palm.

"It recognized you!" Tomoko exclaimed.

"Of course it did. I'm famous."

"Ha," said Tomoko.

The message cube had no obvious lid, and did nothing when Tyler twisted it, knocked it with his knuckles, or tapped it against the ground.

"Maybe it's voice-activated?" Ling-Wa suggested.

"Um . . . play message?" Tyler tried.

"Message begins," said the box, in the thunder-rumbling voice of a Commissioner.

"Greetings, Planetary Captain. We intend this recording to find you as your team completes final preparations for tournament play. Identical instructions have been sent to each of your counterparts across the Pod Gizmo bracket of non-eugenic, pre-singularity teams.

"As you are aware, each season's competition is governed by a unique set of rules, generated by the Commission. For this season, Pod Gizmo teams will compete in a split-squad format."

"A what?" Tyler felt like an idiot for talking back to a recording, but the program must have anticipated his question. A new hologram appeared above the message cube, looking like a constellation of about three dozen specks of light.

"These stars represent the thirty-six players and one planetary captain of your team," said the cube.

"That handsome one over there must be me," El Gatito declared.

"You are to divide your team into six squads. Each squad will consist of a squad leader plus five other players. The method of selection is up to the planetary captain alone." The thirty-six points of white light arranged themselves into six smaller groups. The new constellations then turned red, orange, yellow, green, blue, and purple, each with one especially bright star in each group to represent the squad leader.

All six constellations orbited around a thirty-seventh point of light that blazed the brightest of all. "Is that supposed to be me?" Tyler asked.

"Affirmative," said the cube.

Tyler rolled his eyes. Why did robots and message cubes always say "affirmative" and "negative" when they really meant yes or no?

"The planetary captain will coordinate all six squads as they compete against different opponents," said the cube. "Captains will also compete in one-on-one challenges. Please note that Planet Earth's home games will take place on surrogate worlds, due to security concerns and a lack of adequate facilities."

"That makes us sound like some backwater world where aliens aren't welcome," said Felix. "Way to ruin our planet's reputation, Seclusionists!"

The star pattern turned into a Commissioner's swirling black cloud. "Captain Tyler of Earth, please identify your six squad leaders."

"Right now?" Tyler asked.

"Please identify your six squad leaders," the holographic cloud stated again.

"Can't I sleep on it?"

"Please identify your six squad leaders."

"Aargh!"

The other players waved their hands and jostled for Tyler's attention, shouting reasons why they should be chosen.

Tyler decided to steal a play from Felix's playbook. "Okay, let's be fair about this. Everyone who's been to the Moon and back, please step forward."

The other players went silent as Tomoko, Ling-Wa, Felix, El Gatito, and Weez stepped forward.

"And if you've ever defended Earth in an officially sanctioned game against real live aliens, please step forward."

The Challengers each took another step. El Gatito flashed Tyler a wicked grin. Felix and Weez high-fived. Ling-Wa's eyes sparkled with an inner fire.

But Tomoko had gone pale. She trembled like she'd just taken an ice bath.

"You can do this," Tyler whispered.

"How?" she whispered back. "I'm not like you, Tyler-san. You never worry about messing things up. You never worry about anything."

"Of course I do. I just don't let it stop me."

Tomoko swallowed hard and nodded. "Okay. I can do this. Thanks, *Sempai*."

"That's five squad leaders," Tyler announced.

"Noted," said the message cube.

"I just need one more." A rush of would-be leaders pressed forward, but Tyler's top choice was not among them. She also wasn't hanging back with the players who were avoiding eye-contact to not get picked. Tyler finally spotted her by herself, off in the distance, leaning against the carved ball court wall.

There were shouts of protest from his team, but Tyler ignored them as he jogged over to the wall.

Maja looked up at him and sighed. "Have you come to gloat over your victory? To seed the ground with salt? To slaughter the livestock? To pillage the townsfolk? To make awful Viking-based metaphors?"

"Er, no. I've come to offer you a job. How would you like to be a squad leader?"

"Me?"

Tyler shrugged. "You've already been running your own squad, and you played well today. Besides, you've got all that Viking blood coursing through your veins."

Maja shuffled her feet. "My dad's an accountant and my mom runs a bakery. My blood is more a mix of red ink and confectionary sugar."

"But if you go back far enough, there's probably some Viking in there too, right?"

Maja scoffed. "If you go back far enough, everyone's got a share of warrior blood. And whatever my ancestors might have done with a battle-axe, that didn't rub off on me. I'm nothing special."

"You're special on a snowboard," Tyler told her.

Maja laughed. "Oh sure, I can shred my way down a mountain of soft-packed powder, but other than that I'm just an ordinary kid with big buck teeth."

"Someone once told me there's no such thing as an ordinary kid. The job is yours if you want it."

Maja studied his face. "You're not joking."

"I'm not joking," Tyler confirmed.

"Then I accept." She wiped the tears from her face. "I will be the best squad leader you've got!"

The message cube crackled back to life. "Squad leader selection has been recorded as follows: Red Leader Tomizawa Tomoko; Yellow Leader El Gatito Grande; Orange Leader Felix Hoffmann; Green Leader Bei Ling-Wa; Blue Leader Luiz Rafael Vila Lobos; and Purple Leader Maja Fredriksson. Please confirm if this selection is correct."

Tyler nodded. The colors seemed fine to him. "Confirmed," he told the cube.

"Quantum upload pending. Pending. Pending. Upload complete. This message cube will now self-destruct."

"Wait, what?"

Maja backed away as if the cube in Tyler's hand

had suddenly become a live grenade, while Tyler looked around for somewhere to safely toss the thing away—except that everything within in his throwing range was part of an ancient, historic, unique, and sacred Mayan ball court.

"Self-destruction in approximately three cycles," the cube announced.

Three cycles! A bead of sweat ran from Tyler's forehead. "How many seconds is that?"

"Forty-six million, eight-hundred-fifteen thousand, two hundred and eight," the cube stated.

"Oh." Tyler froze in place with the cube in a throwing position over his head. "Really?"

"This unit will self-destruct gradually over the next eighteen months of Earth time. It will slowly break down into a nutrient-rich compost that is beneficial to most forms of plant life. To receive the maximum benefit, place multiple cubes at least three edge-lengths apart in your garden or agricultural field. Message ends."

The holograms blinked out, and the lifeless cube turned from green to brown.

"Wait," said Tyler. "Your self-destruct mechanism is *composting*?"

Maja laughed. "Who would have thought aliens could be so green?"

17

CAMP GALAXY, SASKATCHEWAN:

Ffargax became a Grellian slime-serpent and slid in tight circles through the grassy underbrush around Daiki's limp body. "Oh man, oh, man, oh man, what do I do now? How can I make this right? And why can't humans dissolve into a convenient liquid form so others can hide their bodies? That's just common courtesy!"

Ffargax felt his membranes becoming soft and pliable, and took a moment to pull himself together. "Think, Ffargax, think! The human body has sponges to take in oxygen, and a muscle group to stretch and squeeze the sponges like a meat-based wind instrument. If that system can be repaired, Daiki might be all right."

Ffargax wrapped his serpent coils around Daiki's chest and compressed the lungs until a breath escaped through Daiki's nose and mouth. That was good, except that new air didn't rush in to replace what had gone out.

Ffargax flicked his forked tongue in annoyance. "Do I have to do everything myself?" He unhinged his jaws, clamped them over Daiki's mouth and nostrils, and pumped good air back into the lungs.

Bad air out, good air in. Bad air out, good air in. Bad air out, good air in.

The human boy was breathing again, sort of, but not on his own. Ffargax kept the routine going as he tried to figure out what else was missing.

The circulatory fluids, of course! The fluids needed a pump to keep them moving through the body, and the pump needed a set of electrical signals that were no longer coming through.

A hard reboot would be required.

Luckily, Ffargax's slime-serpent form had a shock-plate that was used to stun small prey. He positioned the plate against Daiki's bare skin and gave a test jolt. The heart beat twice before fluttering to a chaotic stop. Arms and legs tensed and twitched.

Ffargax gave Daiki a second, stronger jolt.

The heart restarted, fluttered again, but this time recovered its rhythm. The beats became stronger and more regular, and the boy took a sputtering breath on his own.

Ffargax detached his serpent jaws from Daiki's face. "I've done it. It's alive! It's alive!"

Daiki opened his eyes, saw Ffargax's serpent form, and screamed.

Ffargax's shock-plate went off and accidentally shocked Daiki into unconsciousness. "Oh, come on! Are you trying to make me hurt you?" He waited to make sure the human boy's heart and lungs were still working on their own before he unwrapped his coils and backed away.

Bushes rustled in the nearby path. "Now what?" Ffargax asked.

A peacekeeper patrol strode into view.

Ffargax formed himself into a mat of turf and dove to the ground to cover Daiki's sleeping form. His underbelly of sod could feel the warmth and labored breathing of the human boy.

"Over here! I swear something just moved!" One of the peacekeepers ran over and stopped with his boots just tickling the edges of Ffargax's grass tips as he waved them with the breeze.

"There's nothing here now," said a second peacekeeper.

"Well there was," said the first. "You heard that scream. And what's with all these boxes with question marks on them?"

"Daiki Shindo is building something out of them."

"The boy with the camera drone? You know, I shoot

a pretty mean video myself. How would I get a job like that?"

"Step one, beat Daiki's high score in the camera drone simulator."

"And step two?"

"Become Tyler Sato's cousin." The peacekeeper laughed. "But seriously, you'd never get that far. Nobody's ever come close to Daiki's high score."

Ffargax lay still and listened as the two peacekeepers called in their incident report: shouts for help, an abandoned worksite, and no Daiki Shindo.

The peacekeepers moved on, and Ffargax shifted back into human form—but this time he chose the height, build, and features of Tyler Sato's cousin. As long as he could stash the real Daiki safely out of the way, Ffargax's new form would serve two purposes.

First, as Daiki, he could reassure the security forces that nothing was wrong.

And second, he'd get closer than ever to an unsuspecting Tyler Sato.

18

The team's return threw Camp Galaxy into chaos. While the squad leaders divided the rest of the players into their new groups, UNOOSA Section Chief Marwa Jelassi dragged Tyler into the trailer that served as her mobile office. "Captain Tyler, am I to understand that your team will be playing on six or seven different worlds at the same time?"

"We'll have six squads and some separate challenges for me as captain," said Tyler. "Or at least that's what the holographic space cube told me, and if we can't trust holographic space cubes, who can we trust?"

"I wish we'd had more notice." Chief Jelassi pulled out her organizer and began scratching out notes with a horribly chewed-on pencil. "That's up to seven sorties at a time with only eight tigersharks in our fleet—a logistical nightmare! With the same number of seats, we'll need more medics, trainers, equipment managers, security guards, assistant coaches—"

"We could have the tigersharks shuttle people in shifts," Tyler suggested. "M'Frozza says the tournament shuttles have special priority in the transport system, so we should be able to get around extra quick."

Jelassi tapped the pencil on the top of her desk. "The tigersharks can't go back for more people. The General Assembly isn't allowing any humans to be left on an alien world without a tigershark gassed up and ready for an immediate return. Not even for a minute." The chief went back to examining her pencil marks. "We could free up some seats by limiting the number of chaperones—but don't worry, I'll make sure your sister isn't one of those who gets left behind."

"I'm sure Amanda would be happy to give up her seat, as long as my Cousin Daiki can still come." Tyler waited for a reaction from the chief, but she just kept twirling her chewed-up pencil. "He can still come, right?"

Jelassi nodded. "What? Oh, yes. He'll have to. He's the only one who can work the camera."

"And because he's my cousin," Tyler added.

Jelassi launched herself back into her paperwork. "Only Daiki's drone can supply a live feed from planet to planet. Which means the other squads will need a media team to film with traditional equipment. They'll just have to bring the footage back to Earth to broadcast it." Jelassi picked up her phone. "Wen! Get me ESPN."

The section chief scribbled more notes, chewed more marks into her pencil, and seemed to forget that Tyler was still even in the room. She hopped back onto the phone and was soon telling the CEO of Nike that there were no longer any corporate seats available on the tigersharks—and no, it didn't matter how much advertising had been purchased, and no, she didn't care about promotional tie-ins, and no, the contractual obligations were not her problem.

Tyler snuck out of the trailer and carefully picked out his path back to the player cabins. But as crazy as the adults at camp were going, the players were ten times worse.

Piles of luggage, clothing, bed linens, and personal belongings filled the space outside the cabins.

Tomoko blocked the entrance to one of the cabins while she yelled at a group of players who were sprawled on the ground in front of her. Knowing Tomoko, she had probably just judo-thrown them all there.

"I claim this cabin in the name of Red Squad,"

Tomoko announced.

"But all my stuff's in there!" moaned a Canadian hockey player who had just been assigned to El Gatito's Yellow Squad.

"Sorry, Kate. You should have thought of that before this cabin turned red."

"Tomoko!" said Tyler. "Let Kate go in for her stuff."

Tomoko rolled her eyes. "Oh, all right. If anyone has personal belongings in the Red Squad cabin, grab it now before it all becomes Red Squad property!"

At the next cabin over, Ling-Wa waved a tentative hand. "Does anyone object to Green Squad using this cabin? If not, that's okay. We could probably sleep outside with the bugs."

Tomoko shook her head. "Ling, you've got to be tougher! Shout! Growl! You're a leader now, so act like a leader!"

Ling-Wa shrank back. "Leaders growl?"

"Or you could try tripping over some rocks. You know, like Tyler does."

"Funny," said Tyler.

"You've done it twice today," said Tomoko. "That's a new personal best!"

El Gatito gave a sharp yank on Tyler's shirt to get his attention. "Captain Tyler! El Gatito needs yellow paint to mark the Yellow Squad's cabin."

"Yellow paint?" asked Tyler.

"Yes! It should be a bold and distinctive yellow, because El Gatito is a bold and distinctive squad leader, but not too dark. Dark yellow looks too much like brown."

"Captain Tyler, over here!" Weez waved his arms to get Tyler's attention. "Tell Felix I need his cabin for Blue Squad because it has the best view of the southern sky. If the aliens who kidnapped my brother ever come for me, it will most likely be from the south."

"I can't trade with Weez," said Felix. "There's a wasps' nest over by that other cabin."

"You're afraid of wasps?" asked Tyler. "I thought you weren't afraid of anything."

"Wasps, Tyler. They swarm like bees, but they don't die when they sting you. They just keep coming!" Felix looked over at the paper nest and shuddered.

Players bombarded Tyler from all sides, shouting so loudly that he could hardly think.

"Captain Tyler!" shouted Noam, the Israeli basketball player. "You've got to remove Fareed from my squad!"

"Captain Tyler!" shouted Fareed, the Lebanese basketball player. "Please remove Noam from *my* squad!"

"Captain Tyler!" someone shouted. "Can we swap

the yellow and green squads?"

"Captain Tyler!" someone else shouted. "Can we switch the red and purple squads?"

"Captain Tyler!" Valya shouted. "Seriously, Fareed and Noam will kill each other if you don't separate them!"

"Cousin Tyler-kun!" shouted Tyler's Cousin Daiki. "I need to speak with you in the most secluded section of the camp. Come with me now, alone and unarmed, giving no thought to your personal security."

"Enough!" shouted Tyler. "Everyone back off and let me breathe!"

The others moved away, except for Daiki. He stood nose-to-nose with Tyler for a moment longer, with his face muscles twitching like bugs under his skin. Finally, he stepped back with the others.

"Thanks." Tyler was in no mood to make any decisions, but there was no getting out of being Planetary Captain. "No players are switching squads, and no squads are switching colors. Departure Day is tomorrow, guys. We all just need to hang on for one more day."

"What about switching cabins?" asked Weez.

Tyler sighed. "It doesn't matter whether you're on the south side of the clearing or the north. Hostile aliens won't be sneaking up on us tonight."

"Not a chance," Cousin Daiki agreed, with an oddly wide grin.

"Can I still get my yellow paint?" asked El Gatito.

"Do I look like a hardware store?" asked Tyler.

Somebody tapped Tyler on the shoulder from behind. "Captain Tyler?"

Tyler spun around. "I said back off!" he shouted, and *sploosh!* A rush of warm, muddy liquid washed over his head and shoulders. Tyler cleared the gunk from his eyes, and saw M'Frozza with three extra-big, extra-wide eyes. Her face-tentacles wriggled like they had lives of their own.

"What just happened?" asked Hari.

"M'Frozza just barfed in Captain Tyler's face," said Maja.

"I did not . . . barf," M'Frozza told the team. "I released my freen glands. It is an involuntary reaction meant to ward off predators."

Tyler dropped his goop-covered face into his hands. Great, now he'd gotten himself so worked up that M'Frozza's reflexes had mistaken him for whatever monstrous creature ate Mrendarians for dinner. "Sorry, M'Frozza. I didn't mean to scare you."

"I was not scared." She popped her nose-holes indignantly.

"I also didn't mean to yell at you."

M'Frozza smoothed her face-tentacles back into place. "No, of course you did not. Come with me, Captain Tyler. Before your team's departure tomorrow, we must inspect the buses." She turned and scrambled over the uneven terrain with her foot-tentacles.

"You're responsible for the bus maintenance now?" asked Tomoko.

Tyler shrugged. "A captain's work never ends." He grabbed a blanket from a pile of bed linens on the ground and wiped the freen from his face before following M'Frozza down the path.

"Come see me when you're done, Cousin Tyler-kun," Daiki called out. "I know you are busy, so I will be quick. Quick *and* painless!"

Tyler wondered what that was all about. Maybe it was because his cousin didn't like to fly, even in an airplane, so he was extra nervous about traveling by tigershark to a whole other world. But even still, that was a strange thing for him to say, especially while rubbing his hands together like an old-time movie villain.

At the tigershark lot, enormous wooden crates were stacked so high and so deep that Tyler could barely see the buses. Dr. Luchenkov, stepped around one of the stacks and pointed a crooked finger at M'Frozza. "You! Alien girl! Where is your technician?"

M'Frozza blinked. "N'Gatu? I do not know. Why?"

"He was to meet me here to load these medical supplies onto the buses."

"All of this is just medical supplies?" Tyler asked.

Dr. Luchenkov narrowed his eyes. "You, young man, should be getting some rest."

"Sorry," said Tyler. "It just seems like these boxes are more of a load than the tigersharks can handle."

The doctor shrugged. "These six piles are the bare essentials for each squad. Those over there are optional items I have ranked in order of importance."

"Will there be any room left for the players?"

"That is not my problem," Dr. Luchenkov snapped. "Your team will not be leaving Earth until I'm satisfied their medical needs can be met." The doctor stormed away, calling back over his shoulder from the edge of the clearing, "And you, Captain Tyler, will not be leaving until I am satisfied that you are back in top condition!"

"Okay, Doc!" Tyler shouted back.

"Technician N'Gatu?" M'Frozza called. "Are you here? The scary Earth-doctor is gone, and you can emerge from your hiding spot now!"

Tyler tapped M'Frozza's shoulder and pointed to a green-spotted purple tentacle sticking out from beneath one of the crates. Silently, he and M'Frozza snuck over to the box and stuck their fingers and tentacle-tips under the edge. "One, two, three," Tyler mouthed, and together they lifted.

From under the box, N'Gatu let out an ear-piercing shriek. Across from him, a human girl sat cross-legged with her hands in her lap. She stood and curtseyed. "Hello, Captain Tyler. Hello, Captain M'Frozza."

"Fortuna?" asked Tyler. "What are you doing here?"

The Caribbean girl cocked her head to the side, as if she were amused by such a silly question. "Mrendarian skin has tiny flecks that glow in the dark.

The fortune tellers on Mrendaria read the patterns to foretell the future. I asked N'Gatu to let me try."

"Speck-reading?" asked M'Frozza. "That is rubbish and nonsense."

"Believers swear by it," said N'Gatu.

"Rubbish and nonsense," M'Frozza repeated. "Did she tell you anything useful?"

N'Gatu wriggled his arm-tentacles and looked directly at Tyler. "Well . . . maybe?"

"My reading was only for N'Gatu." Fortuna stepped toward M'Frozza until her nose touched the Mrendarian girl's face-tentacles. "And I don't appreciate anyone trying to bully private knowledge out of my clients. Good day to you, Captain M'Frozza! And good day to you too, Captain Tyler."

"But— but— I was not— *Soft choking sound of surprise at the back of the throat,*" M'Frozza stated.

Tyler smirked. "Nice one."

"I have buses to load," said N'Gatu, as he and Fortuna escaped in different directions.

Tyler kicked at some rocks. "So, M'Frozza, did you really want to make sure our buses were ready for the tournament?"

"No, I wanted to make sure *you* were ready."

Tyler laughed. "Me? Of course I'm ready. I'm Tyler Sato, planetary champion!"

M'Frozza tapped her foot-tentacles and waited.

Tyler exhaled a huge breath. "Okay, truth time? I'm not ready for any of this, but I have no choice. It's like I'm on a rollercoaster and I can't get off, even if the ride is broken and the car comes off the tracks. Everyone's expecting so much of me! Even if we advance a round or two in the tournament, people will still be disappointed that we didn't go all the way. I'm supposed to be this awesome Galaxy Games superstar, but I'm not. I'm just me."

M'Frozza wriggled her face-tentacles and made a burbling-humming sound. Tyler knew it was her way of thinking hard about something. Finally, she nodded and asked, "May I tell you something personal?"

Tyler looked left and right. He saw only Technician N'Gatu, about fifty feet away, struggling to lift one of Dr. Luchenkov's oversized crates. "Sure."

M'Frozza took a slow breath and let it go. "I have been training to become a Galaxy Games captain since the moment I was hatched."

"*Hatched!*" Tyler exclaimed. "I thought so! Er, I'm sorry. Go on."

M'Frozza nodded. "I am known across the Galaxy as a strong player from a historically dominant world. And yet, the first time I was challenged, I gave up. I chose to fail."

"But only because your world is under quarantine," Tyler reminded her. "You couldn't compete in the tournament without your players."

"That is what I told myself," M'Frozza huffed. "But what if you were in my place instead?"

"Me?"

"I have gotten to know you, Ty Sato. You would do anything for your friends, for your team, or for your planet—you proved that on the obstacle course, just today! If somebody put your team under quarantine, you would recruit a new team. If you had to save your world with your eyes closed and your hands tied behind your back, you would find a way. You deserve to be in the tournament. You are a better captain than I could ever be."

Tyler shook his head. "Thanks for trying to make me feel better, M'Frozza."

"I am not trying to make you feel *better*," M'Frozza stated. "I am only trying to make you feel exactly as good as you are."

Tyler wasn't sure what to think. M'Frozza was his friend, but she was also a Mrendarian, and sometimes it was hard to know what was going on inside a Mrendarian's brain. For example, from across the landing lot, there was a loud crash as Technician N'Gatu tossed one of Dr. Luchenkov's monster-sized crates onto the roof of a tigershark.

"N'Gatu!" Tyler shouted. "That's a spaceship, not a road-tripping SUV. How are you going to keep the crates from falling off?"

"Do not concern yourself, Captain Tyler. Technicians on my planet have an advanced tool for exactly this purpose." N'Gatu reached into his kit and proudly pulled out a roll of silver-gray film wrapped around on a cardboard core.

"Duct tape?" asked Tyler.

"D'Uct tape," N'Gatu agreed. "It is named in honor of its Mrendarian inventor, Supreme Technician D'Uct. On my world, there is no problem D'Uct tape can't solve, and I stake my reputation on it working just as well on Earth."

While the technician D'Uct-taped the crate to the top of the bus, another Mrendarian slid into the landing lot. "Saddle up, N'Gatu!" said M'Frozza's pilot, R'Turvo. "We have more human chaperones to pick up. Take these coordinates."

R'Turvo tossed a glowing red sphere just beyond N'Gatu's reach. N'Gatu stretched his arm-tentacles toward the object, snared it, but lost his balance and tumbled off the roof of the bus.

R'Turvo slapped his foot-tentacles against the ground and laughed.

"Pilot R'Turvo!" M'Frozza exclaimed. "Father-Parent will receive a full report of your behavior."

"I file my own reports, Captain M'Frozza." R'Turvo reached out a sticky arm-tentacle and plucked something from Tyler's hair. "Your father will be duly informed of all incidents of public freen ejection."

M'Frozza's face turned a deeper shade of purple than Tyler had ever seen on a Mrendarian.

R'Turvo flipped his arm-tentacles in a sloppy salute and slid into a tigershark, which shot forward and traced an arc into the sky.

"Goodbye, Captains." N'Gatu waved as he climbed into his own tigershark, and soon he too was gone.

"Don't worry," Tyler told M'Frozza. "There's no way your father-parent would ever believe that jerk's word over yours."

M'Frozza burbled with Mrendarian laughter. "Thank you, Captain Tyler. You are a good friend."

"You too."

Tyler felt much better after talking with M'Frozza. Maybe Mrendarians weren't so alien after all, and he should gratefully accept their wisdom and guidance.

Moments later, a gigantic wooden crate fell out of the sky, trailing streamers of D'Uct tape, and landed with a splash in the middle of the lake.

20

Tyler scrubbed the rest of the freen off in the player showers—after finding his toiletries bag in the Blue Squad cabin—and put on a fresh shirt—after finding his footlocker in the Yellow Squad cabin. Then he ran down the trail to join his team for dinner.

Even as far north as Camp Galaxy was, the summer sunlight lasted deep into the evening. But on this night, a thick ceiling of clouds and a wispy soup of ground-fog shrouded the forest in an early darkness. It reminded Tyler of the nearly-instant nightfall in the story Weez liked to tell about his brother's alien abduction.

As he walked, Tyler even found himself listening for the sound of an approaching spaceship, but he heard nothing but the hoot of a distant owl.

Tyler pressed his heel-switches to light the LEDs on his Falcon Zero-Weights. The steady white beam on his left sneaker worked fine, but the right sneaker refused to do anything but flash a red beacon that turned the fog into a shimmering curtain of disappearing, reappearing, disappearing blood-red color.

Tyler shivered.

The owl called again, closer, and this time it was accompanied by an oddly distorted voice.

"Cousin Tyler-kun!"

Tyler stopped in his tracks. "Daiki? Is that you?" Tyler turned all around to light the forest with his flashing red footwear. "Where are you, Daiki?"

"Over here, Cousin Tyler-kun. Follow my voice."

Tyler hesitated at the edge the trail. To track down Daiki's voice, he pushed through a wall of broad-leaved shrubs as high as his chest. What were the signs of poison ivy again? Shiny leaves? Groups of berries? Flashing red stems?

A twig snapped somewhere off to his right.

Tyler jumped. "Quit fooling around, Daiki!"

"Keep coming, Cousin Tyler-kun. I need to show you something."

"Can't you just tell me what it is?" The shrubs ended abruptly, and Tyler stumbled into an area where tufts of grass stuck up through mounds of dead leaves.

Somebody stepped out of the darkness in front of him. Tyler pointed his flashing red sneaker-light upward into his Cousin Daiki's deadly-serious face. "I know you are the Messenger, Cousin Tyler-kun."

Tyler felt his skin crawl. "I'm the what?"

"The Messenger of the Dwogleys."

"Daiki, you're not making any sense. Now, what did you want to show me?"

"Only this." Daiki's grin widened until it reached from one ear to the other. His teeth became long and pointed, like needles. His eyes glowed like embers and tripled in size. His features melted like wax, with his clothing and skin reforming into a sheet of black scales. His hands turned into claws with sharp, knife-like fingers. And finally, a set of telescoping vertebrae stretched Daiki's head away from his body on an impossibly long neck.

Tyler's heart was revved up for an escape, but his feet remained stuck to the ground. "What are you?"

"My name is Ffargax," said the creature. "And I've been sent to kill you."

21

"What have you done with Cousin Daiki?" Tyler demanded.

"Your cousin is safe," said the shape-shifter. "You are the only one in any danger."

Tyler swallowed hard. "Why? What have I ever done to you?"

Ffargax paused. "Okay, look. I'll be honest. I don't really want to kill anyone, but I can't let you contaminate the Galaxy Games Tournament with your Dwogleys." He advanced toward Tyler with his snapping claws testing the air.

Tyler's feet finally got with the program, and propelled him through the trees, down a steep rocky slope, and across a narrow stream. The sound of Ffargax's snapping claws followed him the whole way.

"There are no structures in this part of the encampment," the alien informed him. "Nobody will be coming to your rescue. Just admit you're the Dwogley Messenger so we can get this over with, okay?"

"I don't even know what a Dwogley is!" Tyler called over his shoulder.

Ffargax flew overhead on leathery wings. He landed directly in Tyler's path. Tyler tried to turn but his Falcon Zero-Weights skidded on the loose rocks and he fell hard to the ground.

"Pathetic," said Ffargax. "Would you have me believe that such a weak and clumsy being could defeat M'Frozza the Mrendarian and Stonifer the Ossmendian *without* help from the Dwogleys?"

"Um . . . yes?" Tyler had gotten some help from M'Frozza and Daiki, but that didn't seem to be what this alien killer meant. "Really, I don't know what a Dwogley is."

"You are a bad liar." Ffargax raised a razor-sharp claw that glinted in the moonlight. He took a step forward, then stumbled. At Ffargax's feet, an oddly-shaped rock jutted upward at just the right angle to be a tripping hazard.

"What's with the rocks on this world?" Ffargax asked. "Do they want to be stumbled over?"

Tyler backed into a thicket of thorny branches, trapped and helpless as the alien assassin resumed his advance. But as Tyler's sneaker-light played across the ground behind Ffargax, more and more of the tripping-hazard rock rose out of the ground with every red and white flash. Within moments, the bulk of it had become a fifteen-foot stone block that towered over Tyler and Ffargax both.

The flashing light ranged over a carved face that consisted of two deep-set eyes and a long nose over two thick lips. "Stonifer?" asked Tyler.

"Hello, Captain Tyler," said the Ossmendian Galaxy Games Captain. "Hello, Captain Ffargax."

"So you're what I've been tripping over all day?" Tyler and Ffargax asked at the same time.

"I had hoped not to be so directly involved in this dispute, but I was defeated fairly in a challenge match. Under the Galaxy Games Covenant, I have a duty to support the Earth captain." Stonifer's stone mouth scowled. "Whether I like it or not." A metallic omniroot snaked out from the underside of his stone body. Its claw held a brass key like the one Tyler had seen earlier in the hands of a U.N. peacekeeper.

"My energy cannon!" Ffargax exclaimed.

"Your what?" Tyler blinked. "Wait, that peacekeeper was . . . you?" That would certainly explain those mysterious blasts of lightning.

"That energy cannon belongs to my spawn-father,

so let me have it!" Ffargax demanded.

"Really?" Stonifer spun the energy cannon on the end of his omniroot. "You want me to let you have it?"

"Yes, let me have it!" Ffargax said again. "Let me have it right now!"

"If you insist." A blast of light from the energy cannon struck Ffargax in the chest, instantly melting him into a steaming puddle of goo.

Tyler felt his breath catch in his throat. "Stonifer! You didn't have to kill him!"

"He's a Ffifnaxian," said the rock boy.

"That's no excuse."

"What I mean is, he's not dead. Ffifnaxian children can bounce back from almost any injury without permanent damage."

"You mean he's a kid?" Tyler demanded.

"Right now, he's a puddle. But he'll pull himself back together in a few pulses, unless I give him another jolt to finish him off." Stonifer aimed the key at the pond of Ffifnaxian goo, which was already bubbling and twisting back into a lumpy shape.

"I can't let you kill him!" Tyler grabbed the energy cannon and tried to yank it aside. Instead, he wound up hanging from Stonifer's omniroot like it was a piece of playground equipment.

The Ossmendian boy raised Tyler further from the

ground until Tyler's face hovered just inches from one of Stonifer's gigantic eyes.

"Let's be clear, Captain Tyler," said Stonifer. "Because you defeated me, my entire planet owes you our loyalty. As you can imagine, most of my people find this to be an intolerable situation. They blame me for our loss, and so my life has become pretty miserable."

"I'm sorry about that." Tyler made a quick glance downward at the goo-puddle. Ffargax was quickly forming at least three new heads and a whole bunch of legs. "Can we talk about the good old days somewhere else?" asked Tyler. "Somewhere safe?"

Stonifer sighed. "You really won't let me kill him? Really?"

"Really."

"Then we probably should get away from here."

Ffargax's three fully-formed heads roared in anger. He pounced like an eight-legged tiger. Stonifer swung the omniroot that Tyler was clinging to, causing Tyler's feet to connect with Ffargax's torso, hard enough to push Ffargax back onto only two of his feet.

"Hey!" Tyler exclaimed. "Warn me before you do that. I almost lost my grip!"

Stonifer shook his enormous head. "I can't believe you were the one who defeated me."

Ffargax flailed six legs and a tail in a desperate attempt to keep his balance. Finally, he fell backward and made a semi-liquid splatter into a pile of leaves.

"We're wearing him out," Stonifer noted. "Ffargax never did have much stamina."

Tyler blinked. "You know him?"

"Ffargax is the Ffifnaxian Galaxy Games Captain." Stonifer's rock lips curved into a grin. "My team played against his team in a scrimmage. We won, of course."

Ffargax took on a shape that looked like a flamingo with dragonfly wings. "Stay out of the way, pebble-breath. This fight is between me and the Messenger."

Stonifer's omniroots tensed like coiled snakes. "Call me pebble-breath again and I will tear you into a million pieces of slime!"

Ffargax glared back. "Refer to my plasmic fluid as slime again and I will carve you into a garden statue."

"This is crazy," said Tyler. "I thought the Games were supposed to prevent violence between worlds."

Stonifer frowned. "This is usually true, but at the moment our best option to prevent violence would be to run."

Tyler held on as tightly as he could as a half-dozen omniroots propelled him and Stonifer across the forested plains, with Ffargax in close pursuit.

22

Ffargax swung through the trees as an Agleterian arborite, tracking Stonifer and Tyler by the sound of their crashing through the ferns, rotten logs, and undergrowth below. Ffargax had never known a blocky stone Ossmendian to move so fast, especially while dragging a human passenger along. Too bad the greatest athletic performance of Stonifer's life had to happen outside an arena!

Ffargax struggled to keep up with his quarry. He'd been through an exhausting day of shape-shifting, and the blast from the energy cannon had sapped the last of his strength. He could feel his tree-swinging arms stretch and melt a little more with every limb he grabbed.

From the treetops, Ffargax saw lights and buildings up ahead. Stonifer was carrying Tyler back toward the main part of the encampment. "Nice try," Ffargax stated, and with a new burst of speed he cut the pair off before *they could summon any more help.*

Ffargax willed himself into a wall of Sontolax sponge, causing Stonifer to flail his omniroots in a desperate effort to avoid a collision. Ffargax laughed. Even a rock-creature could be scarred by the powerful acids in his sponge form.

Stonifer backed off slowly while Tyler dropped down next to him. The human boy fumbled with the energy cannon and came close to vaporizing himself by accident, which Ffargax would have taken as a win.

"Stonifer!" Ffargax shouted. "You should be helping me, not him! I'm the one trying to save the Tournament!"

"By killing an active team captain?" Stonifer asked.

"Okay," Ffargax admitted, "it does sound bad when you say it that way, but . . . Dwogleys! They hate our way of life!"

"Ah, I see. You've been brainwashed."

"No!" Ffargax shouted. "The Earth team isn't supposed to be in the Galaxy Games Tournament. You don't have to believe in Dwogleys to see how wrong that is."

"Or maybe you're jealous because my team made the Tournament and yours didn't," said Tyler.

Ffargax clenched his spongy structure, spurting acid in a wide arc. Patches of soil bubbled and smoked all around him, but Stonifer and Tyler remained safely out of range. "Why would you say that?" Ffargax demanded. "Did the Dwogleys tell you to say that?"

"It just makes sense," said Tyler. "If you had a team in the Tournament, you'd be with them, instead of trying to kill me."

"In the Tournament or on the challenge field, my team could blow your team out of any arena in the galaxy," said Ffargax.

"That's what I used to think," said Stonifer. "The humans are weak, slow, dim-witted, inexperienced—"

"Hey!" said Tyler.

"Let me finish. I'm going somewhere with this. Now where was I?"

"Humans are weak, slow, dim-witted, and inexperienced," said Tyler.

"Ah, yes," Stonifer wobbled back and forth in a nodding gesture. "Humans have no sense of strategy. They take unnecessary risks. They have no clue what's going on outside their own little world."

"Are you finished yet?" asked Tyler.

"Almost," said Stonifer. "They are all these things and more, but somehow, their team outplayed my team. How can you explain that, Ffargax?"

"I've studied the footage. The humans didn't outplay your team. Captain Tyler outplayed you, personally. And he could only have done so by cheating." Ffargax had only been guessing, but he knew he was onto something when Tyler looked away. "See? The guilt is etched on his face! Now maybe the Order is wrong. Maybe he didn't cheat by being a Messenger of the Dwogleys, but he did cheat somehow. And as a Galaxy Games Captain, my duty is to keep the games pure."

"That's my duty as well," said Stonifer. "Which is why I choose to defend Captain Tyler."

"Fine!" Ffargax shifted into a six-legged block of metal with a two-pronged appendage sticking straight up from his back. There were now several rebellious pockets of liquid within his body that refused to solidify, but he managed to keep them hidden from view.

Stonifer took a step backward. "You wouldn't!"

"Wouldn't what?" asked Tyler. "He's a bug with a tuning fork on his back. What's he going to do, de-tune your piano?"

"This is your last warning, Stonifer," said Ffargax. "Move away from the human and let me complete my mission."

"I cannot," said Stonifer.

"Then you will die!" Ffargax struck his fork against the metal of his shell, setting off a loud vibration. Somehow, through sheer force of will, he remained solid for long enough to complete the action.

"That's it?" asked Tyler. "Your big attack was a

musical tone? What were you thinking?"

Next to Tyler, Stonifer screamed as tiny cracks spread across his stone skin.

"Stonifer!" the human boy exclaimed. "What happened?"

Stonifer grimaced. "The tuning bug is native to the Ossmendian homeworld. It has perfected the exact frequency needed to vibrate rock-animals into a fine powder, which it then sifts through for rare elements."

Ffargax readied his tuning fork for another intonation. "Please, Stonifer, don't make me kill you. Leave while you can still fuse yourself back together."

Stonifer ground together the boulders that made up his gigantic teeth. "I would never abandon a friend in need. Of course, I must admit that doesn't mean anything as far as Captain Tyler is concerned."

"Gee, thanks," said Tyler.

"Still, I will stay. My people already hate me for losing a can't-lose game. At least they won't be able to say I was a coward as well."

Ffargax groaned. He really didn't want to kill Stonifer. He liked Stonifer. He thought the Galaxy Games were stronger because of great competitors like Stonifer. But if there was truly no other way to take Tyler Sato out of the Tournament . . .

"Wait!" called Tyler.

"Yes?" asked Ffargax. "Are you ready to confess that you are the Messenger of the Dwogleys?"

"I'll confess to anything you want, just put the tuning-fork away."

Ffargax felt like his brain was swimming inside his head, and it was only partly due to the fact that his insides were slowly melting to liquid. "Are you saying you're the Messenger because you're the Messenger, or because I'm asking you to say you're the Messenger?"

"I'm not sure what that question means," said Tyler.

Ffargax flicked his wings in annoyance. What was the right thing to do? He had no idea. What would Spawn-Father do? Kill them both now, and sort it out later. It wasn't a very good solution, but it was all he had.

"It's not too late," said Tyler. "We can talk this all out. Just don't—"

Ffargax struck his fork again.

At the same time, with a pained expression, Captain Tyler raised the energy cannon and pressed the discharge button.

23

Tyler raised the brass key, aimed at Ffargax, and pressed the button. He then squinted at the strangely unaffected Ffifnaxian. Although Tyler had never fired an energy cannon before, he was pretty sure it should have had some sort of effect.

Directly behind Tyler, a fifty-foot spruce tree burst into flames.

"You idiot!" shouted Stonifer. "You're holding it backward!"

Some part of Tyler's brain registered that if his weapon hand had been a few inches to the left, he would have blasted his own head off. And if he'd come home without a head, his mother would have been really upset. And his father. And possibly even his big sister.

And what about Ffargax? Tyler studied the Ffifnaxian's shimmering bug form. Stonifer had said that Ffargax was just a boy—a shape-shifting, cousin-impersonating, murderous monster-boy, sure, but wasn't it likely that Ffargax also had a family?

"What are you waiting for?" Stonifer asked. "Shoot him!"

Tyler tossed the energy cannon away. "I'm not a killer."

"Then what good are you?" Stonifer shouted.

"Hey, you're not the only one who gets to have a sense of honor."

"True, but *your* sense of honor is dishonoring *my* sense of honor by letting me die for nothing!" The light from the burning tree grew brighter as the fire spread, allowing Tyler to see more cracks appear across the Ossmendian's body. Pieces from his oversized head dropped onto the ground, his stone body crumbled, and even the omniroot tendrils shattered into twisted bits of metal.

Within seconds, nothing remained of Stonifer but a pile of debris.

Ffargax had also lost his shape, oozing into a tired puddle. "Can't sleep yet," the Ffifnaxian's voice bubbled. "Can't sleep yet, can't . . . sleep . . . yet!"

The battle was over, and somehow Tyler was the only planetary captain left standing. He stepped forward and bowed his head over the rubble that used to be Captain Stonifer.

"That's right, just keep standing there," said the rubble. "Don't even think of running to safety."

"Stonifer!" Tyler's heart leapt at the thought that somewhere inside that sarcastic mound of sand and grit, the Ossmendian captain still clung to life.

Tyler dug with both hands, finding pebbles about as large as his pinky finger, and a few more as big as his fist, but none that seemed to have any spark of life within them.

"Just go!" the rocky whisper urged. "And promise that if you ever go to Ossmendia, you'll tell the Elder Council how I defended your life. Even though you were entirely unworthy of my sacrifice. Be sure to emphasize that last part."

Tyler yanked out the largest rock he could find in the pile of Stonifer rubble. It was about the size, shape, and color of a brick and felt warm to the touch, although cooling fast in the misty Canadian air.

Twenty feet away, another spruce tree exploded, adding to the widening ring of fire.

"Stand still, human!" Ffargax staggered forward. He was back in Daiki's shape, except that now he looked more like a melting Daiki robot made from colored wax. The brass key shook and wavered as Ffargax tried to hold it with his semi-solid hands.

Tyler took three steps back and raised his arms. From the sky overhead, the hum of a tigershark engine grew steadily louder: a rescue that was right on time but also way too late.

The tigershark landed behind Tyler. Ffargax's next shot hit the bus, but did no damage. The tigershark door yawned opened, and Tyler scrambled inside.

"Captain Tyler, Hello!" Technician N'Gatu burbled at him from the driver's seat. "I spotted your thermal distress signal while transporting a new chaperone to camp. Effective as it was, you probably didn't have to burn quite so many trees just to get my attention."

"Close the door!" Tyler shouted.

The Mrendarian's face-tentacles wriggled in confusion. "Why? Is there a draft?"

Another blast from the energy cannon shook the tigershark.

"A crazy Ffifnaxian is trying to blast me with an energy cannon!" Tyler shouted.

N'Gatu pressed a button, and the door clamped shut like a giant set of jaws. "I will do whatever you want, Captain Tyler. Just stop waving that brick around."

Tyler looked down at the piece of Stonifer in his hand. He hadn't even realized he was still holding it. Another blast hit the bus. Through the window, Tyler could see the goopy Daiki-shaped figure stumbling closer, outlined against an acre of burning evergreens.

"Get us out of here!" Tyler shouted.

"Where should I go?" asked N'Gatu.

"Anywhere but here!"

Technician N'Gatu pushed a lever forward in front of him, and the tigershark lurched into the air.

Tyler sprawled to the floor in the aisle of the bus.

"Apologies!" said Technician N'Gatu. "Evasive maneuvers weren't part of my flight training. Setting the navigation to 'anywhere but here.'"

"Destination randomizer engaged," stated a computerized voice inside the dashboard.

"Randomizer?" Tyler asked. "Why would a navigation system need a randomizer?"

"It was part of the original specs."

Tyler picked himself up and checked to make sure Stonifer's brick-shaped remains hadn't cracked. "Can you land us by the administration building? If we alert the peacekeepers, they'll be able to capture Ffargax before he causes any more trouble."

"Well, I *could* have done that." N'Gatu twisted two of his arm-tentacles around each other. "But when you said *anywhere but here,* I assumed you weren't limiting our destination to your own world."

Tyler blinked. "So we're going back to the Moon?"

"Probably not so close as that." The Mrendarian's face purpled from grape to plum. "The random places inside your solar system are very few, while the random places outside your solar system are very, very, very many."

"We're leaving the *Solar System*?" Tyler slumped into the nearest seat. "This is not how I wanted to become the first human being to visit an alien world."

"One of the first two human beings to visit an alien world," said Technician N'Gatu.

"One of the—" Tyler frowned.

"I did mention that I was transporting a new chaperone to camp," Technician N'Gatu stated.

Tyler slowly turned to scan the seats behind him. His big sister, Amanda, sat in the last row of the bus with a book in hand and her sandaled feet up on the seat back in front of her.

Amanda shook her head. "Honestly, Ty. I don't know what nonsense you're burbling about with that squid-thing friend of yours, but do you really have to act like your life is one big adventure story with cliffhanger endings and 'To be continued' printed at the bottom of the last chapter? It's just *so* annoying!"

To be continued ...

GALAXY GAMES

The Mad Messenger

Coming in 2017

from Spellbound River Press

SpellboundRiver.com

AUTHOR'S NOTE

When I spoke at schools this past year, there was a moment in my talks when the classroom went absolutely silent. It came right after I explained that Galaxy Games is about a group of kids who represent Earth in a sports tournament against kids from other worlds.

In that moment of silence, I could tell that every kid in the audience was imagining what it would be like to represent an entire planet. Our planet.

And then the hands went up.

Some hands waved urgently, others were more tentative, but the question was always some variation of this:

"Does your team include somebody like me?"

I love when I can say yes. Yes! In books, someone like you can do amazing things. And in real life, *you* can do amazing things. Because Earth needs heroes

166

like you, just like you, to get into the game.

That's why it was so important to me that I got this opportunity to expand the Galaxy Games series with more books, so I could write about more members of the team and say yes to even more readers. Especially readers who don't usually get to see themselves in books, going out into the universe, having heroic adventures, playing sports at the highest level, or simply being recognized for their efforts and abilities.

This is where I need your help. If you have comments or questions about Galaxy Games, drop me a note through my website or through my publisher. Tell me what you want to see in future books. Let me know the parts you enjoyed most, but also what you think I could do better.

I hope these books inspire you, because you've inspired me to write them.

Greg R. Fishbone
www.gfishbone.com
May 2016

ABOUT THE AUTHOR

As a kid, Greg R. Fishbone was a voracious reader of science fiction and fantasy. His early influences include Douglas Adams, Piers Anthony, Madeleine L'Engle, and Ursula LeGuin. He began writing with friends as a hobby, making a game of continuing and finishing each other's stories. Over time, he gained the skill and confidence to write and finish stories of his own.

Greg published his first book, *The Penguins of Doom*, in 2007 and teamed up with other debut authors of that year to form the celebrated Class of 2k7. Greg serves as Assistant Regional Advisor for the New England region of the Society of Children's Book Writers and Illustrators.

He and his wife are raising two young readers and a pair of stubbornly-illiterate cats in a half-acre suburban patch of Planet Earth.